SAVE WHISKERS!

A HUMOROUS THRILLER

STEFON MEARS

Also by Stefon Mears

The Rise of Magic Series
Magician's Choice
Sleight of Mind
Lunar Alchemy
Three Fae Monte
The Sphinx Principle
Double Backed Magic
Mercury Fold (coming soon)

Cavan Oltblood Series
Half a Wizard
The Ice Dagger
Spells of Undeath

Power City Tales
Not Quite Bulletproof
No Money in Heroism

Standalones
The Hireling (forthcoming)
The Captain's Cat (Forthcoming)
Save Whiskers!
The Ogre of Threepeaks
Between the Cracks
Sects and the City
Prince of a Thousand Worlds
Devil's Night
Portal-Land, Oregon
Stealing from Pirates
Fade to Gold
With a Broken Sword
Twice Against the Dragon
The House on Cedar Street
Sudden Death
On the Edge of Faerie

Short Story Collections
Spell Slingers
Twisted Timelines
Longhairs and Short Tales: A Collection of Cat Stories
Dangerous Space
Confronting Legends (Spells & Swords Vol. 1)
The Patreon Collection, Vol. 1-8 (Vol. 9, coming soon)

Nonfiction
The 30-Day Novel and Beyond!

Spells for Hire Series
Devil's Shoestring
Zombie Powder
Spirit Trap
Dragon's Blood

The Telepath Trilogy
Surviving Telepathy
Immoral Telepathy
Targeting Telepathy

Edge of Humanity Series
Caught Between Monsters
Hunting Monsters

Jumpstart Duchy Series
Into the Torn Kingdoms
The Dragon's Gold
The Gift Castle
The Deadly Feast
The King's Test
Triumph in the Torn Kingdoms

Published by Thousand Faces Publishing, Portland, Oregon

http://1kfaces.com

Front cover image © Benchart | Dreamstime.com (File ID: 50302947)

ISBN: 978-1-948490-51-1

SAVE WHISKERS!

PROLOGUE

Whiskers was having trouble finding the right sunbeam. Which was strange in and of itself. Sunbeam detection had always been one of his gifts. Like an instinct. As clear and obvious as the scent of a mouse or the chirp of a bird.

Yes, he was young. Hardly more than a kitten. He knew that. But ever since he'd first opened his eyes, he'd known how to find the good sunbeams.

And yet, even though his internal clock told him that dawn and dusk were almost equidistant, and that the sun should be high and strong overhead, all the sunbeams were weak.

They were weak in the softest sleeping room. They were weak in the chatty rooms, where the two-legs all meowled in serious voices.

Whiskers didn't like the chatty rooms. The two-legs could get very territorial in those rooms. Making either low, harsh sounds at each other, or even their loud, dominance sounds.

Not as effective as a good strong yowl, in Whisker's opinion, but the best the two-legs could manage. And big as they were, Whiskers never liked to stick around those chatty rooms. Never knew when the territorial sounds would start and the feet would clump about heavily.

Times like those, the anger in the room smelled like burning metal, and ruffled his fur from the tail on up.

All the same, he'd checked every one of the chatty rooms today. Just in case.

Hadn't helped. No good sunbeams in any of them. And not in the food room. Or any of the several good lounging rooms.

No, Whiskers knew he finally had to go where he knew the two-legs really didn't like him to go. Not that he understood their displeasure. This was *all* his territory. He'd marked it himself, on the cold morning when they'd moved in. That day when he'd smelled the frozen water for the first time.

Whiskers had still been a kitten that day, but even then he'd been a proper cat. He'd known the importance of marking what was his. Places, of course, but the important two-legs as well. Such as the three two-legs he'd marked back when he first met them. When his eyes had barely been open. The three most important two-legs in his life, and the source of much love, joy, and comfort.

Rumble Laugh, and Sweet Voice, and Whiskers' favorite, Nuzzle.

Nuzzle was smaller than the other two. Perhaps their kitten. She smelled right to be their kitten. But she was the most affectionate, and more than happy to pick up Whiskers and try to nuzzle him properly every time she saw him. Even though she seemed unfortunately bereft of proper scent glands.

Well, Whiskers had made sure to mark her *thoroughly*, to make up for the deficiency that wasn't really her fault, after all. All two-legs seemed to lack those scent glands, poor things. How they ever marked what was theirs, he didn't know.

But Nuzzle certainly knew how to scritch all the best places just right.

Unfortunately, not one of his three favorites was around that day — the day the sunbeams were off — and that was strange too.

Well, Nuzzle was often gone until mid-afternoon. But Rumble Laugh spent most of his days in one chatty room or another. Dealing with pride matters, most likely. He seemed to run a very big pride. Given the number of two-legs he meowled at daily, and the deference he received from others. Why, sometimes, he'd have dozens of two-legs coming to him at a time! And not always the same ones!

Quite a pride indeed.

But if Whiskers poked his face up, even when Rumble Laugh was busy, it usually meant a joyous moment of that wonderful rumbling laugh, some soft mewls in his deep, deep voice, and a little petting, before the two-legs started meowling at each other again.

Which was when Whiskers usually made himself scarce.

And Sweet Voice, she was almost always around here somewhere. She had her own pride matters to deal with, it seemed, but she also...

Well, to be honest, Whiskers was never quite sure what Sweet Voice was doing with her time, most days. She always had other two-legs around, but they weren't as often engaged in serious meowling like with Rumble Laugh. And frankly, no matter how much Whiskers watched her, a lot of the things Sweet Voice did didn't make any sense to him.

But whatever it was she did, she seemed happy enough about it for the most part. If Whiskers could find her, even when she was busy, he'd usually get a good scritch. If a brief scritch.

Though usually that scritch was followed by being picked up by one of the rigid two-legs, and taken from the room.

Then a door would shut. Which was pure *effrontery*. Whiskers usually gave that closed door a good long yowl, before collecting his dignity in a quick bath, and moving on to someplace he'd be *appreciated*.

But that day, they all three were gone like the good sunbeams.

Whiskers never liked it when his favorite two-legs were gone. Not easy to look after them, to keep them safe from the kinds of threats they could never guess at, when they were away from his domain.

But he could do little to stop them, when they were determined. They were much bigger, after all, and they knew how to make doors open for them.

There was a similar device attached to every door in Whiskers' domain. Round. Shiny. Whiskers had watched while the two-legs used their forepaws to make them turn. Though sometimes even they couldn't turn the device, and needed to jab it with something, to make it behave. *Then* it would turn for them.

Whiskers wasn't long enough, yet, to reach that device. But he would be one day. And surely his claws could jab well enough to make the silly round things open for his paws.

And when that happened, Whiskers would be Master of Doors. Then the two-legs couldn't keep him out of *anyplace*. And maybe he'd be able to chase his three favorites, when they were foolish enough to leave his domain…

Ah, a pleasant future to consider over a quick drink of sweet water and snack of fresh, minced sardines in the food room. And the best thing to follow a good snack, while considering wonderful possibilities, was a good sunbeam.

If only Whiskers could find one.

Well. No help for it. He'd have to go into the Bird Viewing Room.

Oh, that was a good room. Whiskers wasn't supposed to go in there, though. Rumble Laugh and Sweet Voice had both made that clear. And at those times when Whiskers slipped in there anyway, inevitably one of the lurking rigid two-legs would scoop him up and whisk him from the room the moment they spotted him.

Well, sometimes they'd chase him from the room, when Whiskers didn't feel like letting them pick him up. Either way, though, it amounted to the same thing. Eviction, and closed doors.

The nerve.

That was the room where Rumble Laugh would stand behind a tall, wooden place to put his forepaws. The tall thing smelled like linseed. When he stood there, a great many yowly two-legs would come in and mass together to thrust forepaws toward him and yowl for his attention.

When that was happening, well, Whiskers didn't like being in there anyway. Too noisy. And too many of the two-legs smelled funny. Like fake flowers or fake leather or fake some other thing. Plus, on most of those days, they closed the curtains and took away the transparent wall.

No fun at all.

But when the room was empty, and the curtains open, he *still* wasn't allowed in there. Which was *entirely* unfair.

Nuzzle, at least, seemed to understand this. And agreed with him. She'd sneak him into the room sometimes, when it was empty. And the two of them would flop before the transparent wall and look at the grass, and the maples and elms. And even better, they'd watch the birds and squirrels flit and bound about.

Whiskers could catch a bird. Or a squirrel. Or maybe one of each, for good measure. If only he had a chance to hunt one…

He could go in that room now. Sunbeams had to be good, in front of that transparent wall.

And no one else was around. Not even the two-legs who *always* lurked about. Smelling as rigid at they stood, and hiding their eyes behind those black things that perched on their noses.

They were all off doing something too.

So where was the harm?

Wouldn't hurt anyone for Whiskers to wander in there. Lounge on sun-warmed hardwood in a good sunbeam in front of the transparent wall. Maybe watch a few birds and squirrels. Maybe even chatter the Summoning Sound at them…

Whiskers looked about one more time first. Making sure no lurking rigid two-legs had escaped his notice, ready to swoop down and scoop him up indignantly.

But he seemed to be alone.

So in he went. Moving on the softest of soft paws. Evading the obvious sight lines, just in case a wandering rigid two-legs happened by.

Whiskers made his way over to the transparent wall. But the floor wasn't as warm as it should've been. And even here, where the sunbeams were at their *most* reliable, that day's sunbeams were weak.

Why, they were no stronger than typical, early morning sunbeams. Gentle, yes. Warming, after a fashion. But not the good, blazing, melt-into-a-happy-purring-puddle kind of sunbeams that should have been easily available at that time of day.

Really quite frustrating. And there was no one around to soothe

Whiskers' frustration. No familiar lap to jump into and demand scritching. No laughing, eager attention from a favorite two-legs as much in need of distraction as Whiskers was himself.

But distraction did come for Whiskers that day.

Not in the form of a sunbeam or a friendly lap.

And not from a favored two-legs.

No, not from any two-legs Whiskers knew at all.

1

Oregon summer days could be downright nasty, when they wanted to be. We didn't get much rain during the height of summer — believe it or not, Portland does *not* live in a perpetual downpour. Unlike, say, Seattle, from what I hear — but there were days the air got so thick with humidity it was like being wrapped in hot, wet towels.

Right down to the extra weight.

My feet felt slow. My arms felt slower. And adding in the heat blazing down through air so thick it probably refracted enough light to throw a sundial off by an hour or more?

Forget it. Only an idiot or a madman would be out for "fun in the sun" on a day like today.

But let's be honest here. In the summertime, all Portlanders — probably including all Oregonians, and possibly even all denizens of the PNW — go a little mad, and a little idiotic. Flooding the streets and rivers and highways and parks in a desperate attempt to enjoy the sun before it vanished again like a gopher, frightened of its own shadow.

And me, I was probably a little madder — and every so often a little more idiotic — than even most of my fellow Oregonians.

So yes, even though the sun was blazing, and the air was so thick with humidity that it smelled like a wet dog on the verge of mildew, I was out here of my own free will. Doing something that would drive my doctor crazy, if I told him what I'd been up to. Which I wouldn't. Unless I had to.

I was playing soccer.

For those of you who don't know, soccer probably falls just shy of motorcycles as the leading cause of stupid knee injuries. And amateur soccer is probably even worse in this regard, because we who play it don't get fancy, professionally groomed and leveled fields to play on.

No, we idiots and madmen who dared the heat and humidity to run about like children chasing a ball, we had to play in public parks. Which weren't nearly as well-tended.

But the smell of grass and good sweat. The feel of muscles working hard enough to give a little lactic acid burn. Of lungs and heart pumping even harder, maybe. These things made me feel alive like I didn't most days. Since I'd retired, anyway.

Oh. Yeah. I suppose I should point out the other reason my doctor would consider slapping a twenty-four-hour commitment on me for being out playing soccer on a day like this one.

I wasn't a spring chicken anymore. And over the years, while working, I'd picked up a couple of lingering injuries that, if they acted up the wrong way at the wrong time, could shut me down for a week.

But life was for the living. And I wasn't ready for a life of little more excitement than gardening and visits to the Saturday Market.

Hell, I wasn't even sixty yet. I had *decades* to go. Assuming a moment of madness or idiocy didn't take me down.

That day, we had enough players for a full eleven-on-eleven, and a few people ready to sub on, in case of mischance. We even had proper gloves for our keepers, and nets to fill the goal frames. If we'd had a crowd watching, the experience would've been complete.

The game was Shirts versus Skins — amended to include sports bras, for the women on the Skins team, of course. I was playing midfielder for the Skins.

My preference, in terms of teams. I knew some of my old scars would intimidate the kids half my age. Especially since I still had better muscle tone than most of them. And while yes, I'd lost some of the speed I'd once had, I still did enough daily long distance running that I had the endurance to keep up with all of them, and outpace more than a few.

All right. I admit it. One reason I enjoyed playing soccer was that, when the old injuries didn't interfere, I *could* more than hold my own against kids half my age.

Which I was doing right then.

The Shirts had overcommitted on their last attack, and now we were on the counter.

Steve, our right winger, had the ball and was reminding everyone that he ran the hundred meter for U of O during the school year. Bringing the ball up the right side, outpacing the woman marking him, and smart enough to keep his eyes up.

Andrea, our striker, was making a run down the left-hand side. Holding back just enough to keep herself on-side. And she was where we wanted the ball to go. If Steve gave her a good pass, she could ditch the man marking her and go one-on-one against their keeper. A sure bet for our side.

Me, I was going full-steam down the middle of the field. Making a run, yes, but I wasn't expecting the ball. Really I was just forcing their two centerbacks to mark me — or at least not ignore me — and give Andrea a little breathing space for her attack.

Best part about it for me? I really was going full-steam. But I'd learned long ago how not to *look* like I was going full-steam. My top speed was barely enough to push past their midfielders and center-backs, but by looking like I had more to give, waiting for the right moment to give it, I demanded even more attention than they wanted to pay me.

Getting scored on by an eighteen-year-old Latina who would kit up for OSU this fall? That wouldn't embarrass anybody.

Getting scored on by the old white dude with all the scars? That was another matter entirely.

Steve made his pass too early. Should've waited another five steps, but I logged that to inexperience. He was a sprinter by preference, not a soccer player. I was pretty sure he was out here to show off his trim physique for the girls.

His pass looked pretty good, at first. Nice arc...

Short. Way short. Must've hit it at the wrong point in his stride. That ball was coming down maybe halfway between me and Andrea.

Andrea saw that the same moment I did. Our eyes caught, and I gave a quick nod to the right.

She didn't acknowledge. There wasn't time. Instead, she cut right and turned up her speed.

Huh. I hadn't realized how much she was holding back. I hoped the Thorns — our local National Women's Soccer League team — were scouting her.

She pulled not only her trailing marker, but the nearer of the two centerbacks. His mistake, that centerback. Gave me just exactly the edge I needed.

I cut left, going for the ball.

The one centerback still marking me — a thirtysomething guy carrying a few extra pounds — cut too. But the angle was better for me, and he was slowing down. And I was already faster than he was. Gave me about three steps lead, and growing.

I reached the ball before it got out of bounds. Glanced toward Andrea as I got to it. She was already reaching the eighteen-yard-box — still onside, barely, because she was cutting more horizontally than vertically — but their winger and the other centerback both trailed her by at least two steps each...

Steve was running faster still. Must've reached his full sprint speed. Cutting toward the goal box. Making a threat that kept the keeper's focus split, worried about where I'd send the pass.

I didn't waste time dribbling. Moment I reached the ball I fired off a cross with my first touch, coming off my left — and stronger — kicking foot.

The cross was good. Came in right for Andrea, in stride.

But their keeper must've faked me. He wasn't worried about Steve at all. He was already moving to snag Andrea's header.

But Andrea was smarter. Didn't send her header for goal. She dropped it right at Steve's feet.

He caught it in stride and put it in the back of the net.

We were celebrating our goal when I realized that back behind the net — where we stored our stuff during the game — I could hear my phone ringing.

And it was a ringtone I hadn't heard since I'd retired. A ringtone I hadn't realized I still had on my phone.

A ringtone that meant real trouble.

2

______

REAL SOCCER DOESN'T HAVE TIMEOUTS. THE CLOCK KEEPS MOVING, AND if anything delays play by the time they reach halftime or full time, additional minutes — called stoppage time — gets added to make up for lost playing time.

But let's get real. We might've been playing eleven-on-eleven and mad enough — or idiotic enough, depending on whom you asked — to be out here playing in conditions that would make a steam room ask if we wanted to reconsider, but we were still a bunch of amateurs.

And when I heard that ringtone, I stepped right away from the goal celebration and yelled, "Time out!" Even made the time honored time-out symbol with my hands, before I trotted around the white netting of the goal to get my phone.

Naturally, I hadn't even reached the phone yet before the "There's no time out in soccer!" bitching began. Honestly, made me consider giving them a time-out gesture formed of only two, very specific fingers. But I knew it wouldn't help.

I just turned away from the complaints — one of which included someone pegging me with an open plastic water bottle, which was both littering and a waste of perfectly good water — and dug through the pile of stuff for my phone and keys.

Because given the ringtone I was hearing, I knew I'd need both.

I answered the phone as soon as I could get it to my ear.

"This is Hank Sauer, response code Charlie Alpha Hotel two four two."

"Good. Sorry to—"

"Counter code, please," I said.

Yes, I recognized the voice. I knew full well that that was DeeDee Morrison, the woman who'd taken over for my old boss at the Agency. (No, not *that* Agency. Though I think technically we might have been a branch of them. I know our funding came out of their budget, someplace.)

I'd seen DeeDee rising through the ranks. Solid analyst, and even better running things behind the scenes.

But that wasn't the point.

"Since when are *you* a stickler for protocol, Sauer?"

"Since you interrupted my soccer game. I'm *retired*, you know."

"Read your contract again. You know we can un-retire you in times of sufficient need."

Ah, yes. "Sufficient need." I knew the clause well. I'd fought over the years to get that damned phrase *defined* someplace, but never could get anyone to commit to a solid, written definition.

Which meant that it was either a sign of my madness, my idiocy, or my patriotism that I'd continued to serve my country anyway, right up to retirement. And apparently beyond.

I, of course, preferred to think of it as a sign of my patriotism. Most days, anyway.

Andrea strode over to stand in front of me. Forty feet of angry Latina, packed into a five-foot, leanly muscled frame. She flashed dark eyes up at me.

"What the fuck, Hank? We've still got ten minutes to go." She clapped her hands at me. *"Vamanos!"*

I held up a forestalling hand and shook my head, lips tight to show I wasn't messing around. And I lowered my voice as I said into the phone, "Counter code, or I'm going back to my game."

"Fine," DeeDee said with a dramatic sigh. "Counter code Mike India Alpha One-Seven-Seven."

We use a complex set of codes at the Agency — excuse me, *used*, since I *was* retired. They changed by season, following a certain pattern that all field agents had to memorize.

And the code DeeDee just gave me, spoken by the home office at the height of summertime, meant the worst kind of news. A problem involving the White House.

"What do you need?" I said at once, waving away the angry Latina who was now snapping at me in Spanish and tapping her wrist.

"We need you here as soon as possible."

"I need to swing by the house for—"

"You don't."

Whoa. Whatever it was was a big enough deal that they'd handle *everything*. They'd have clothes and weapons for me. They'd have someone feed my cats Sturm and Drang. Change their litter. Play with them.

That also meant my ride was waiting at the airport...

"I'll hop the MAX train out to—"

"Your ride will be pulling up by the time you reach the street. Get moving, Sauer."

I looked over my shoulder at the stormy sea of soccer players — joined, apparently, by more spectators than I'd known about, all of whom wanted me back on the field.

"Sorry, guys. Emergency. I've got to go *right now*."

That stunned most of them into silence — I'd never abandoned a game before — but some of them heaped disbelieving derision on me anyway.

Even away from the game, the park was pretty well packed. Three barbecues were smoking up what smelled like enough burgers and dogs to feed the entire Portland metro area. Kids ran and screamed at one another, while blasting each other with water guns strong enough to have kick.

Enough happy dogs chased Frisbees and kids that the fastest path to the street meant hurdling two picnicking couples — one of which didn't even notice me — and cutting across midcourt of a five-on-five basketball game.

I reached the curb just as my ride pulled up. I knew it at once, of course. It was a big, nondescript hybrid SUV covered with all kinds of liberal bumper stickers that ensured it would be all but invisible on Portland's streets.

Anything *that* perfectly ordinary only happens by design.

I hopped into the front seat before the SUV came to a halt, and it started picking up speed again even before the blasting freon crystallized my sweat and sent shivers right down to my bones.

Driving the car was a guy about my age. Japanese heritage, his short black hair not showing any gray, and his Portland disguise perfect. Sandals, cargo shorts, Timbers tee shirt, some kind of fitness watch on his wrist.

"Don't remember offering you a ride," he said, giving me a dark look, even as he shifted lanes to take us toward a freeway entrance.

That was a code phrase. Despite what bad spy movies might've led you to believe, the best code phrases don't sound like code phrases. They sound like things real people might say.

(Or reasonably close, at least. I mean, most people would've been a little more panicky if a big, scarred stranger jumped into their vehicle.)

"Figured you owe me," I said, giving the countersign. "After I gave you that ride home from Pioneer Courthouse Square last week."

He nodded. "Sauer?"

I nodded.

"I'm Yamato."

Yamato? That had to be David "One Shot" Yamato. Never worked with him before, but I knew he'd been with the Agency almost as long as I had. Taken retirement only six months before I did. Supposed to be an absolute badass with just about every kind of firearm and blade ever made.

"You just doing them a favor? Or did they—"

"Reactivated me for this." He gave me a small smile. "Looks like we'll finally get to work together."

"I'm torn," I admitted. "On the one hand, I'm glad I'll have One Shot watching my back. On the other, now I'm really worried about how big this is. They tell you what's going on?"

"Nope. I don't think they even trust our secure phones with ... whatever it is."

I whistled softly.

"Exactly," he said.

"Mind if I call you David?"

"David's fine. One Shot's fine too, long as you don't sound sarcastic about it."

"Wouldn't dream of it," I said. "And call me Hank."

"Pleasure, Hank," he said, offering one hand to shake as he pulled us onto 84 East, toward the airport.

"Good to meet you," I said.

He had a good handshake. Steady. I hoped his gun hand was still just as steady. I had a feeling we'd need it.

3

———

Should be pretty obvious that David and I weren't going to be flying commercial out to Washington. Not in an emergency situation like this.

No, this was a big enough deal that they sent us the ride to end all rides.

Air Force Four-and-a-Half.

Obviously, that's not a call sign you're going to find on Wikipedia, or hear mentioned on the news. It's just an Agency nickname.

The call sign doesn't officially exist.

And neither does the plane itself.

It's not much bigger than a fighter jet. Looks kind of like a fighter jet, to be honest. Except that it's painted a dangerous shade of sky blue. And it does have the stars and bars on it — painted in two places that I knew of, and both places only a slightly darker blue, so as to be almost invisible while still *technically* present. Much like the plane itself.

I wonder sometimes what air traffic controllers call that plane. If they call it anything, other than "the nightmare" or maybe "the boogeyplane."

See, those poor air traffic controllers never know when it's going to show up, when it's going to leave, or where it's going. All that information is strictly need-to-know, and they don't qualify. But they're still stuck with clearing the sky for its takeoff and landing.

And with a paint job like that, they need to clear a *lot* of sky around it. To avoid ... mischance.

Worse, they don't get to explain the resultant delays to the airlines, let alone the passengers.

Ever suddenly find that your flight was just postponed sixty to ninety minutes for no discernible reason? Maybe you looked up at the screen and saw a whole bunch of planes getting delayed at the same time.

Yeah. Sometimes that just happens. It's true. But sometimes, just sometimes, it's because our government needs to give someone an emergency high-speed ride on a plane that doesn't officially exist.

And that day, David and I both qualified for such a ride.

David, since he was driving, must've been told in advance. I, on the other hand, only found out when he avoided the parking areas and drove us out onto the tarmac.

I'd been about to ask when I spotted the three fuel tanker trucks on a runway *way* off to one side, well away from most of the gates.

Three fuel tanker trucks suspiciously placed, to block the right kind of sightlines. Say, while waiting for us.

Nerves began percolating in my stomach, and demanded I seek confirmation.

"We're taking Four-and-a-Half?"

"Yep," David said. "Hope you didn't just eat lunch."

I shook my head. Admittedly, I was starving. My bacon and eggs were hours past, and I'd done almost ninety minutes of full-pitch soccer with kids half my age. (Some even younger than that.) And I'd had to trot past all those delicious smelling barbecues, just dripping with dogs and burgers, chicken, maybe some steak...

I shook away the images and focused on the chill of the SUV's air conditioning to get my mind off food. David was right. At the speeds we'd be flying, an empty stomach was better.

We came around the end of the tanker trucks, and there it was. Air Force Four-and-a-Half.

Oh, how I hated that thing.

Girding myself for an unpleasant time, I hopped out of the SUV as soon as David put it in park, and welcomed the blitz of blistering sun on my skin. Of which I still had a lot showing, since I was only wearing athletic shorts and Nikes.

David exchanged passphrases with a young woman wearing a maintenance jumpsuit, and she hopped into the SUV and drove it away.

"Hurry up, you two! Burning bridges here."

That would be the pilot. Some young Navy or Air Force hotshot on the kind of special assignment he'd give his left nut to be able to talk about in bars.

Burning bridges? Oh. Right. The entire airport was waiting.

David smiled, and gestured to the ladder.

With a sigh, I climbed the ladder, donned my helmet, and squished myself in the seat behind the pilot. David, a moment later, took the last seat and helmet for himself.

David, though, was shorter and skinnier than me. He was strapped in and signaling ready while I was still trying to get the harness around my torso.

The tapering sides of the plane pressed in on my shoulders. Like always. My knees were wedged into the seat in front of me. Like always. Felt like being packed into a jack-in-the-box. Add in the too-loud hiss of the breather — necessary since we wouldn't have cabin pressure — and the chemically cold taste of its air, and I knew I was in for the kind of fun ride that really felt like a warmup for waterboarding. Or maybe someone yanking off my fingernails.

I fought the even-more-restrictive harness into place with a harsh click and said, "Ready," into the mic.

"Tower," the pilot said over his radio. "This is three-three-one-one-seven-two, ready for takeoff."

No, three-three-one-one-seven-two was not the plane's designation. It was the pilot's.

"Proceed when ready, three-three-one-one-seven-two."

The tone was formal. The "good riddance," only implied.

"Here we go," the pilot said.

The whine and rumble of the engines coming to readiness always made me imagine being at the heart of a huge volcano at the moment of eruption.

Honestly, it was the best part of flying in this thing. Enough of a thrill that I could forget my sheer physical discomfort for a short time.

We started forward.

After only a moment, even our groundspeed was enough to press me back into the seat.

Then we took off. And not at a slow climb. Oh, no. Nothing so innocent and fun as that.

No, we curved into a vertical ascent. While building speed.

Which means we were pulling multiple gees already, and this was still the warm-up part of the trip. The part of the rollercoaster where you're climbing, and you know the real speed is yet to come.

I don't know how high up we flew. I know it was high enough that the sonic booms we'd generate wouldn't mean much more than a car backfiring back on the ground in Portland.

Do cars even backfire anymore? I mean, why is that even still a saying?

Just a sign of how desperate I was to think about anything else, rather than what was about to happen. That I'd waste time wondering about something like cars backfiring, when deep down I knew what was coming.

Hell, my stomach was already dropping, and my ears were popping like a kids' cereal.

Because we leveled off.

The pilot whooped as he put the hammer down.

Look. I know I'm not a kid anymore. All right? I'm the first to admit it. (Well, maybe second, because my doctor is faster to say it than I am.)

But nothing reminds me that my skin has lost some of its youthful springiness like passing Mach seven.

My face was rippling like a pool after a cannonball.

I'm pretty sure my stomach dropped out back somewhere over the Cascades. I spent pretty much the whole crushed-in, too-fast flight focusing on taking long, slow, deep breaths of that chilly, chemically air.

The whole way, of course, the pilot was blasting hard rock like he was starring in some big-budget action movie. The music helped, though. His taste was pretty good, for the modern stuff. Disturbed, Shaman's Harvest, and The Pretty Reckless.

As for our total flight time, well, the plane exists for a reason. Didn't take us thirty minutes of total time in the air before we were touching down at Reagan Washington Airport.

4

———

There are different kinds of "situation rooms" under the White House. Some of them are really big. Like the ones they need for war or natural disasters that threaten the Eastern Seaboard. Others are of a more moderate size. Accommodating maybe twenty people in relative comfort.

This situation room, though, was much smaller. In fact, I think anywhere else, it would've just been called a conference room. And not a big one at that.

But this was the White House. If going into politics meant living under a microscope, then working in the White House meant living under the kind of microscopes that could tell you what an electron had for breakfast.

Everything here was historic. And anything that happened *under* the White House proper, well, that pushed past historic and threatened the doors of legendary.

So everything got fancier names, fancier titles, fancier coffee.

Seriously. The brew I was holding — in an official White House cup, that probably had to be saluted for its service when it went into the dishwasher. Assuming it wasn't washed by hand, by an aide chanting the pledge of allegiance — smelled like rich roasted heaven, and tasted even better.

I think that when coffee beans are little, only a small percentage of them are smart enough to even *dream* of growing up to produce coffee this good.

Then again, maybe those are the stupid ones. Maybe the smart ones dream of growing up to do whatever it is that unpicked coffee beans do. Grow more coffee plants?

Anyway, to go with Heaven's Best Coffee — patent pending, I'm sure — there were cookies that had to have been baked to someone's idea of perfection.

But not mine, I can tell you.

They were chocolate chunk, not chocolate chip, and they were too well done for me to taste the richness of the baked dough.

Damn it, chocolate chip cookies — *good* chocolate chip cookies — were more than just a chocolate delivery system. They were a full tasting experience. And that only came when the cookies were at least a little soft, so the butter and brown sugar of the dough could properly set up the punch of the chocolate chips.

They should also, preferably, be served warm and moist. But that was a lot to ask. At least, when I wasn't baking them myself, and had the option of starting in on them as soon as I damn well felt like it.

Honestly, I was half-tempted to dunk a cookie, to see if it would help. But I suspected...

All right, all right! I knew *full well* from *past experience* that it is considered against protocol to dunk one's cookies in the presence of the POTUS.

Of all the times I'd been chewed out over the course of my ... colorful ... career, that was the strangest. Getting yelled at over *how* I'd eaten cookies during a briefing with the president.

Anyway.

Of course, coming into the presidential presence wearing nothing but shorts and sneakers was frowned on as well. But on this front, I was safe. DeeDee had proper clothes waiting for both David and me soon as we unwedged ourselves from Air Force Four-and-a-Half.

We'd changed in the back of the Hummer on the way from the airport.

Now we looked pretty slick, for a pair of old dudes. Gray suits. Gray ties. Black loafers and belts. Shoulder holsters (empty in this room, of course). Work phones. We actually almost looked like we belonged at an important table like this one.

The room itself wasn't all that much larger than the black oak table. Thin, blah brown carpet over concrete, and neutral dove gray wallpaper on the walls. Light glared down from an overhead LED lamp. Smelled like they'd just cleaned in here too, and used too much bleach. Flags in the corner, of course, featured Old Glory and the presidential seal.

Like we could possibly forget where we were.

For a fairly small conference room — excuse me, *situation* room — it was pretty well packed. Down at my end of the table, DeeDee sat at the foot, with me on her right and David on her left. Between us and the other end were suits of both sexes — none of whom I recognized, but that didn't mean much, because they were the younger people present and likely aides of some stripe — but close to the end were people I recognized.

Chief of Staff Monica Andrews, with the take-no-prisoners bearing that doubtless made White House workers tremble at the thought of messing up. Deputy Chief of Staff Darnell Collinwood, who had a deceptively gentle bearing, for a big man. Secret Service Director James Buckminster, who wasn't much wider than a .45's barrel, and whose eyes never stopped moving. FBI Director Ellen Markov, who looked about as happy to see me and David as I'd been to board Air Force Four-and-a-Half.

And at the end of the table, of course, the big man himself. President Miles Martin. Tall. Regal. Deep voiced. Skin darker than Wesley Snipes. And the kind of sheer presence that could hype up a football stadium to raucous levels without his ever saying a word.

At the moment, he looked like contained fury. And the containment was slipping, because I could feel his fury almost like a weight against my skin. Itched. Made even me want to shift about.

I didn't, of course. Way too well trained for that.

And I'll tell you. Even if I *hadn't* once been yelled at for dunking cookies in the presidential presence — that's right, it had been more than one — I wouldn't have risked it right then. Just in case these cookies were done to President Martin's preference.

No way *I* wanted to become an outlet for this man's fury.

"What do you know already?" Chief Andrews asked.

"They—" DeeDee started, but Andrews interrupted her.

"I asked *them*."

I swear, the temperature in the room dropped five degrees.

David and I looked at each other.

"Sauer," Andrews said. "You first."

"At approximately eleven-seventeen hours, pacific standard time, I received a call from—"

"I didn't ask for a history lesson. I asked what you know about the current situation."

Wasn't like President Martin's rep to let people snipe at each other that way during meetings. I mean, I hadn't met the man, but he was known as a peacemaker and a brilliant negotiator.

Which made me worry all the more about what was wrong.

"Nothing except that something big has happened. Something big enough to pull myself and David Yamato out of retirement and fly us across the country at great speed and great expense."

"And you don't know what?"

"No, ma'am."

"Yamato?" she said.

"No, ma'am. I have nothing to add to what retired agent Sauer has already said."

Andrews opened her mouth to say something. She never got the chance.

"Then I'll tell you myself," President Martin said. "Someone has stolen my cat."

5

———————

Presidential pets have a long and varied history. Starting with Washington's personal pack of dogs that included three staghounds, all the way through the more modern stars like Socks Clinton and Barney Bush.

But none of them captured the country's hearts like little Whiskers Martin.

The Martin family didn't have a pet during the presidential campaign, and when a reporter asked about that, then-candidate Senator Miles Martin smiled his famous smile and said, "I promised Shonda that when the election was over, we'd get her a cat. Win or lose."

The magic started right then. From an offhand question directed to a candidate on his way out to dinner with his family.

Little seven-year-old Shonda Martin, barely in the shot, looked right into the camera and said, "And my daddy *keeps* his promises."

That clip didn't just get plenty of airplay. It became an internet sensation. And not just as a good moment for a campaigning politician.

I don't know if you've realized this, but people on the internet go *nuts* over cats. And between Miles Martin's charm and his daughter's earnestness, Whiskers was a major story before he was even born.

After the election — which Martin won in a landslide — the questions came about when and where he would adopt the cat. Whether he'd go to a breeder, whether he had a specific breed in mind, all that kind of thing.

When President Martin announced that they'd visit animal shelters and cat rescues just before New Year's until "a cat picks us," his approval rating went through the roof. And the guy hadn't even been sworn in yet.

Cameras followed the President-Elect's family to those shelters and rescues. The whole nation got to see that tiny orange kitten light up at the sight of them and leap straight into the arms of a crouching Shonda, who squealed in delight.

Whiskers suited the Martins, I have to admit. Charismatic and photogenic as the new first family. Courageous. Inquisitive.

The nation *adored* him. His social media feeds had more followers than the President's. He even had his own version of Roosevelt's famous Fireside Chats. Every Friday evening, Whiskers played with a dangling feather toy, and tens of millions streamed it. Live.

And now, someone had stolen him.

It was a Sunday afternoon. That meant we needed to have Whiskers back before Friday, or the whole country would know he was missing.

Bad enough. But worse was the implication that some foreign power might be able to get agents into the White House. If they could catnap with impunity, what else could they do?

I didn't need any time to connect the dots here. I did it as soon as President Martin announced the problem. Training, yes, but over the years I'd proven to have an instinct for seeing future consequences.

At least ... for *other people's* actions.

So no sooner did President Martin make his pronouncement in that small, gray conference room — excuse me, *situation* room — than I said, "So we've got fewer than a hundred and twenty hours to get him back before all hell breaks loose."

Beside me, Agency Director DeeDee Morrison made a small sound of approval, and David gave me a nod of support.

Around the black oak table, my clear, simple statement of the situation set most of the suits at ease. Not just the younger ones I assumed were aides. Chief of Staff Andrews and Deputy Chief of Staff Collinwood looked relieved at my immediate understanding.

But Secret Service Director Buckminster still looked uneasy. Maybe because it happened on his watch. Then again, if that was his problem, why didn't Deputy Chief of Staff Collinwood feel just as uneasy? He was, arguably, even more responsible for the lapse that allowed the catnapping.

More important to me at the moment, though, was this. I didn't know what, specifically, I'd done to piss off FBI Director Markov — I swear, I'd never met the woman before. At least, not that I remembered. And I was pretty sure I'd remember a woman that big and angry — but she continued to glare at me as though I were personally responsible for not only the catnapping of Whiskers, but also the price of gasoline, and any problems her personal stock portfolio might be having.

Or maybe those chocolate chunk cookies were baked to *her* idea of perfection, and she could tell I disagreed. Some people picked the weirdest — and wrongest — hills to die on.

But President Martin, he didn't look either relieved or angry. Not at me, anyway. No, he still looked like a thunderstorm held back by a fraying sheet of gauze. But he nodded once, briskly, before saying, "That's true, Agent Sauer. But I want to be clear about something. I am not, in this instance, worried about public reaction. I am not worried about implications. And I am not worried about political fallout."

He leaned forward.

"I am worried about Whiskers. And I am worried about Shonda, who is missing her pet even more than Janice and I do. She is a child, and Whiskers is her first cat. A cat I also happen to love a great deal. And I want that cat home safe and sound *as soon as humanly possible.* Do I make myself clear?"

"Absolutely, Mr. President." The words came out be reflex. Which was good. Because in person, the man's presence was staggering. If I'd had to think, I probably couldn't have *forced* a word out.

"If I may point out, sir," Director Markov said, "that isn't *Agent* Sauer but *Retired* Agent Sauer. I have a great many agents capable of handling this matter. Agents whose training and skills are *current*, and whose records—"

"No one's impugning your people, Ellen," President Martin said, though his focus was still on me. Like a rolled-up newspaper, hovering, ready to squish a spider.

A simile that pretty much drove Director Markov's point home, in my opinion. I mean, most of her agents probably weren't old enough to *remember* newspapers as something that arrived every day, printed on paper, and got used to kill spiders.

But I didn't have time to pursue that line of thought. President Martin was still speaking.

"However. DeeDee raised a good point this morning, and I agree. Better to keep this operation off the books. That'll give our agents room to maneuver, and minimize the number of eyes on them."

"If that's your preference, sir, then..." Director Markov said at the same time that Director Buckminster said, "The Secret Service has 'secret' in the name, sir, and..."

The president cut them both off with a wave of his hand.

"I have already considered and rejected both your proposals. We're going with DeeDee's plan. And you both have to admit. Sauer and Yamato here are each responsible for a good number of very quiet victories for this country."

"They managed a *few*, sir, yes," Director Markov said, "but Sauer's record—"

"Enough," President Martin said. Not with force. Not with volume. But with this air of complete finality. As though by his word alone, all other possible arguments and points of dispute were simply ... eliminated.

And it worked. Both Director Markov and Director Buckminster simply nodded in acquiescence.

Neat trick. Wish I could do it.

"Sauer, Yamato," President Martin said, "you are both retired. And I understand that your contracts give me the *right* to call you back into service. But I consider this more of a personal matter than a presidential one. So I'm not going to force you. If you want to say no, you will suffer no fallout and face no consequences. You will be compensated for your time and returned to your homes either with maximum speed or maximum comfort, by your choice."

He leaned forward a little.

"In other words, I am not ordering you to do this. I am asking you, one human being to another. Will you find my cat and bring him home?"

I didn't even hesitate. "Of course I will, sir."

Hell, I'd've done this if it'd been a neighbor's cat. I'd been a cat lover all my life, and looked at catnappers the way the Old West looked at horse thieves.

The president and I both turned to David, who was frowning as he considered.

"You're not required to say yes to this," President Martin reminded him.

"I understand that, sir," David said. "And I want to help. It's just, well, I'm more of a dog person, and I'm worried Whiskers will smell that on me. He needs to be confident in his rescue team."

"I've had three dogs over the course of my life," President Martin said, "and I loved them very much. The last one died just before Shonda was born. I've always thought of myself as more of a dog person than a cat person. But I can assure you, Whiskers doesn't hold it against me."

"Then I'm happy to help, sir," David said with a nod. "But Hank should probably handle Whiskers when we find him. Just to be on the safe side."

6

———

The White House is never completely empty. Ever. No matter what's going on, or how many big events are pulling the important people out to this meeting and that function and that other thing, there's always *someone* there.

The Secret Service has people guarding the entrances and exits — interesting fact here. Not all White House entrances are exits, and not all White House exits are entrances. Except, maybe, in the Shakespearean sense, I mean — and there's usually a few staffers around.

Oh, I don't mean aides, in this case. Well ... all right ... there are usually at least a few of those around too. But I'm talking about staffers. The nonpolitical — though not necessarily *a*political — folks who handle the food, the cleaning, and those other sorts of duties that have to get done every day.

Believe it or not, there are no magic elves that keep the White House running.

Well. All right. I can't really *swear* to that. I mean, I've never seen any, but if they're magic elves, maybe I wouldn't. You know? Plus, it's not as though I've searched every room of both wings, and all of the basements and subbasements and grounds. For all I know, there *is* a secret cabal of magic elves that have a *lot* of say in keeping the White House running. Maybe even in the kinds of policies that finally get approved.

What can I say? I've heard stranger things than that. Some of which have proven to be true.

My *point* is that, if there *are* any magic elves in or around the White House, they don't do the cooking and cleaning. That's done by actual human beings. I've seen them. Talked to them. And at any given time, there are probably about twenty of them somewhere in the building. More if you include butlers, doormen, gardeners and the like.

So while it's true that, on the Sunday morning that Whiskers was catnapped, the White House was *almost* empty, it wasn't *completely* empty.

True, it happened to be the one day a year when all of the political folks were off at churches or fundraisers or having official meetings or "playing golf" — which was code for having *un*official meetings — or something similar. And with them went a good portion of the Secret Service agents who were usually roaming the White House, or standing around looking tough and official.

In *that* sense, the White House had been empty all morning.

But empty, for the White House, meant that there'd been a dozen Secret Service agents on duty and — according to the logs — six members of the nonpolitical staffs, apart from the Chief Usher herself.

Now, in my nearly three decades of service, I'd been to the White House in an official capacity dozens of times. And in my experience, that number of Secret Service on duty for an "empty" White House sounded about right.

But only six of the nonpolitical staff were in the building? Including both wings?

That sounded *way* low to me.

So once the smokescreen of paperwork was finished — giving David and myself official status that people couldn't ignore, without officially designating us as anything, which is the kind of maneuvering you only found in places like the District of Columbia — the first person I wanted to talk to was the Chief Usher.

The White House Chief Usher was an elegant woman named Crystal Mackintosh. She was sixtiesh and slender, and had been serving in the White House for more than a dozen years. The kind of woman who managed to project the airs that Europeans thought of as suggesting noble heritage and Americans thought of as coming from old money.

But true to her position, she didn't feel unapproachable. She struck me as the kind of person who could handle just about any problem with swiftness and aplomb, while directing all eyes back where they should have been in the first place, so it became as though the problem — whatever it was — had never occurred.

She wore a simple black suit, and her silver hair back in a ponytail as crisp as my tie. Most interesting, she had a small scar on the back of her right hand that I was dying to ask her about. The kind of scar most people would mistake as coming from some kind of accident, and would believe almost any story about.

But I knew scars. Had plenty of my own. And that one had come from having a stiletto jammed into the back of her hand at just the right angle to catch on a bone.

Frankly, I was impressed that she appeared to have full use of the hand.

David and I met with her in her office, which looked like what I'd expected as soon as I'd met her. Simple. Understated. Little personality showing, because that would be a distraction for guests. But two, silver-framed pictures on her maple desk. One of a smiling, gray-haired chap in admirable condition who I figured to be her husband.

The attractive young couple with the happy little kids in the other picture would be her ... daughter's family. The mother in the picture had the same smoke gray eyes as Ms. Mackintosh. Which was how she preferred to be addressed, she informed us, as she invited us to sit in the spartan chairs on the other side of her desk.

"Ms. Mackintosh," I said, "we've already read over your statement and those of your staff."

"Very good," she said with a nod. "I'm pleased I shan't have to repeat myself."

"You've all been quite cooperative," David said. "We appreciate that."

"My staff fairly dotes on the cat. Not one of us would see a hair of its fur harmed."

"Glad to hear it," I said. "But this was a strange morning, wasn't it? I mean, a lot of people must've called off work, for your staff to be so light today."

"Not in the least," she said. "No one sought to be excused due to illness or personal matters of any kind. Everyone whom I expected to be here today was here promptly, and has done everything asked of them."

"But only six people?" David said, picking up as though we'd rehearsed it. "That's rather below normal for a Sunday morning, wouldn't you say?"

"It is one-fifth of the normal complement. But sufficient to the tasks I required of them this morning."

"Surely you must see," I said carefully, "that it looks a little suspicious. That the very day that you have six people doing the jobs of thirty *just happens* to be the day that little Whiskers gets catnapped."

"I most certainly do *not* see that it looks suspicious," she said in tones that could've given my marrow frostbite. "And I resent the implication you seem to be making."

"I'm not implying anything," I said. "I'm saying it looks suspicious."

"And he has a point," David said. "Certainly it would be a heck of a coincidence."

"I do not pretend it is coincidence. But you've committed two important errors in your logic."

"And those are?" I asked. And for the record, I wasn't insulted.

Here's the thing about errors. Whether they're accidental or deliberate, they'll often teach you a whole lot more than you expect.

"You stated that I asked six people to do the work of thirty. I should hardly need to say that I did nothing of the sort, but it appears I must be explicit here. I asked six people to come in this morning. The six most junior of their relevant positions. All individuals who had been serving here for less than a year. And I assigned them such tasks as would make sure that at least the absolute minimum of necessary work would be completed before one o'clock this afternoon." She arched a silver eyebrow. "Or thirteen hundred hours, if you prefer."

"Do you do this often?" David asked.

"I do it precisely once each year," she said. "On a date that is scheduled well in advance. And I presume that I must now explain the whys and wherefores?"

"If you'd be so kind," I said.

"It is not a matter of kindness," she corrected me. "So much focuses on the political work done in this building, that the general public" — she arched that judgy eyebrow again — "including those I would expect to know better" — she settled back in her seat — "forgets that the nonpolitical workers are under no less pressure than their political counterparts."

"I'm not sure that's true," David said with more tact than I could've mustered.

"I guarantee it," Ms. Mackintosh said. "This is the *White House*, gentlemen. Everything here must be pristine. Every door opened at exactly the right moment, and closed again swiftly, smoothly and silently. Every meal served promptly and at its proper temperature, regardless of any delays or last-moment additional guests. Every room must look picture perfect at all times, because at any given moment it may be immortalized in historical record."

She looked about as though she could see through the walls. "Every inch of both wings must be perfect at every moment of every day. Anything less will be subject to ridicule, and an embarrassment to both this administration and this nation."

I whistled softly. "That does sound like a lot of pressure."

"Which is why I make sure that everyone under my command

avails themselves of their benefits. And by that I mean not only their annual vacation time and sick leave, but also their medical care, for themselves and their families."

"Wonderful," I said. "But what does it have to do with this morning?"

"I was coming to that. As my personal thank-you for all their hard work, on one day each year and at my own expense, I send my people and their families for a day of entertainment. They vote on what it will be. This year they have chosen a trip to a rather popular water-park. They have it all to themselves, and all food and drink is catered."

"And they have to be back by one?" David asked.

"They do not," Ms. Mackintosh said as though David were stupid for asking. "There are always a dozen or so who disappointed by the results of the vote. So I offer them a half-day off to spend as they choose, and some other, shorter activity on a different date. In this case, they will be attending an upcoming game of the Washington Nationals."

"And they're the ones arriving at one," I said. "Sounds good for everybody but the junior members of the staff."

"If they have not worked here a full year, they have not yet earned the treat," she said simply. "If, next July, everyone has worked here for a full year, I will have temporary workers vetted to fill the need."

"So this special fun day," David said. "You say it was scheduled months in advance?"

"Of course," she said. "A great many schedules must be coordinated."

"So," I said with a sigh. "The staff would've been talking about this day for months with family and friends."

"Easy date to find out," David said, shaking his head. "Is it always on a day when the political staff is so conspicuously absent?"

"Usually not to the degree they were absent this morning, but yes. Such days tend to see fewer immediate needs." She looked at me. "Will that be all? I do have duties."

"We'll get out of your hair," I said, a phrase she must not've liked. Given the set to her mouth when I said it.

As David and I left her office, he said, "So much for a quick answer."

"Ah, 'the usher did it' has a terrible ring to it anyway."

7

Unfortunately, the interview with the Chief Usher was more productive than our interviews with the Secret Service agents who'd been on duty at the time of Whiskers' catnapping.

Or as I started thinking of those agents, the Twelve Angry Men.

They were angry about a lot of things. They were angry that Whiskers had been stolen. They were angry that it had happened on their watch. They were angry that they were stuck here, and not out trying to find him. They were angry that they hadn't been allowed to leave or even contact anyone, because they believed it meant they were under suspicion.

Which, of course, they were. And they were angry about that too.

Most of all, though, they seemed to be angry at David and me in particular. Two old guys they didn't know — even though I remembered at least two of them, and I was pretty sure David recognized a couple as well — were being given an investigation that "by all rights" should have been theirs?

Better believe they were angry about that. And being angry at the president wasn't all that smart, when you work for the Secret Service, so they were angry at us instead.

Yep. For all of it. Every bit of the anger and frustration they were feeling that day. All of it. Every crumb of it. Every *iota* of it. All directed straight at David and me.

Yeah, those interviews were fun.

They all went about the same way, too. So I'll sum up. Give you some idea of just how much fun David and I were having with those guys.

Imagine, if you will, a little white concrete room, three floors below the White House grounds. A room the president probably doesn't even know about, because no one wants to be the one to mention it.

Stuffy little room, because the air conditioning gets spotty in here, and smells like dust and decay. A room where the floor has some rather suspicious looking old brown stains that never quite come clean. Probably by design.

Those stains are exactly what they look like. And let me tell you. Even having them in my peripheral vision during those interviews was enough to produce the olfactory memory of blood's metallic tang.

There's one table in the room. Old steel, painted the color of ancient, forgotten tanks, and bolted to the floor, so no one could flip it to use as a shield. Or a weapon.

No one had given as much focus to the creaky wooden chairs. But that was because most people getting interviewed in this room had their hands cuffed to the table.

Not so for the parade of all but identical men David and I had to interview that day. They weren't confined. The only concession to their status being that they'd been disarmed, both of their weapons and their communications. No guns, no knives, no phones, no radios.

Just a whole lot of anger. And training. And youth.

Not that I was worried. If these kids were stupid enough to try anything, either of us could eat them for breakfast and still be hungry.

There's a reason we were the two called out of retirement for this.

We didn't want to fight these kids, though. They had a right to their anger.

If they were innocent.

Unfortunately, innocent or not, when it came to answering questions, they weren't all that cooperative.

Here's a sample.

Me: What time did you arrive this morning?

Angry, Sullen Man in Dark Suit: I arrived exactly on time for my shift, as scheduled.

David: And what time was that?

ASMiDS: That time is registered in the logs.

Me, growing irritated: Do you own a watch?

ASMiDS: I do not.

David, holding his temper better than I was: I can see one on your wrist.

ASMiDS: A smartwatch is part of our standard uniform, and must be worn at all times while on duty. But I, myself, do not own a watch.

Me: Do you know how to *use* a watch?

ASMiDS: A wristwatch?

David: *Yes*.

ASMiDS: A wristwatch is used by turning one's wrist and reading the time as displayed, presuming either that enough ambient light is present to make this possible, in the case of an analog wristwatch, or that the watch battery currently contains sufficient charge to display the time, in the case of a digital wristwatch. If you mean to ask how a *smart* wristwatch is used, that answer will become more expansive, as it depends upon the brand and the apps installed. Do you require instruction in how time is read from a wristwatch, either analog or digital?

Those were real answers, by the way. And each of those Twelve Angry Men was just as informative about everything. Even the kinds of establishing questions we needed to ask, to create a foundation for the more important questions.

Maybe that cooperating-without-cooperating thing was just anger. Maybe it was resentment that they weren't the ones doing the investigating.

Or maybe it was all a smokescreen to protect someone.

Unfortunately, whatever the reason, we didn't learn much from those Twelve Angry Men *except* that they were angry. And, it seemed, that right up until the discovery that Whiskers was missing, at approximately one-forty-seven p.m. Eastern Standard Time, not one of them had witnessed anything out of the ordinary that day.

Nor had they left their posts except at appointed break periods (which were also in the log, apparently). Nor had anyone entered or exited the White House through the doors they guarded, except as logged.

By the way. There'd been *no one* entering or leaving the White House between about nine a.m. and one p.m. Not that any of these Secret Service agents told us so. No, David and I had to learn that from the logs.

Once we finished the last of those interviews and stepped out into the hall, Secret Service Director Buckminster was waiting for us.

The hall felt like a bunker. Fluorescent lights not quite steady. Stale smell to the cold air. Acoustic tiles on the ceiling, and white concrete on the floor and walls.

Here, away from the president, maybe, Director Buckminster looked dangerous, for a little man. Like he'd gotten to where he was by personally assassinating everyone in line ahead of him.

Even now, his eyes didn't stop moving. Now looking at my face. Now David's. Now checking one direction. Now noting my pistol under my left shoulder. Now the knife concealed against my left shin. Now checking the other direction. Now noting David's knife, concealed along his right forearm. His pistol under his right shoulder. The area behind him. Back to my face.

Every one of those quick glances got repeated throughout our conversation, but not in any discernible, predictable order.

"Well?" he asked, in a tone of pure expectation.

"Your men aren't very cooperative," David said.

David, of course, being the soul of tact. I ... was a little more blunt.

"Who are they protecting?"

"They protect the president, of course." Buckminster arched an eyebrow. "I presume you're familiar with our mandate?"

"Are you suggesting that the president stole his own cat?"

That got a moment of dissonance from Buckminster, who shook his head hard to clear it. "What nonsense is this?"

"Your men," David said, shooting me a warning look, "have been singularly uncooperative with our investigation."

"Are you suggesting that my men have lied to you?"

"No," I said. "We're suggesting they've been obfuscating. I presume *you're* familiar with the word?"

"What my colleague means," David said quickly, drawing the director's attention back to him, "is that it's unusual for innocent men to be so wholeheartedly uncooperative with an investigation."

Buckminster's eyes focused on me for a moment, as though memorizing my features in case he needed to sneak into my window one night.

I stared right back at him. So he knew that if he tried it, I'd be ready.

After approximately one thousand three hundred forty-seven years of that stare, he turned back to David.

"It's bad enough that this happened on their watch," he said, eyes moving constantly once more. "Now their competency, honesty, and patriotism are being called into question at the same time."

"So they circled the wagons while trying to figure out if one of them did it?" I asked.

"No," Buckminster said, fully in control of himself again and looking more like a director of the Secret Service than an assassin. "They know none of them did it. But this kind of investigation could produce side charges. Especially if Whiskers is not found, or ... let's just say not found in the state we hope."

The mere thought of what he was implying was enough to start some fiery anger of my own down in my guts.

"Anything they say now, innocuous as it may be, might be used against them later. So they protect themselves by replying with only provable answers."

"Such as references to the logs?" David asked.

"Precisely so."

"Nevertheless," I said, "that may be innocent behavior as far as you're concerned—"

"I did not say it was innocent behavior. I am merely providing the most likely explanation for it and denying that it is necessarily *guilty* behavior."

"Then I presume you won't try to contradict us," I said, "if we insist that they continue to be held incommunicado for the time being?"

"You should run your investigation as you see fit, of course." He gave me a considering look. "Is it now my turn in that small room?"

"I currently have no reason to believe that will be necessary," I said, sounding sufficiently diplomatic that I could feel an implied lift to David's eyebrows that he declined to show on his face.

I didn't need the interview, though. Not at this point. We already knew Director Buckminster wasn't present this morning. At least, not according to the logs.

Besides. I wanted him thinking he wasn't under suspicion. He'd looked more than a little uneasy earlier. And if the Twelve Angry Men were protecting someone other than the president himself with their behavior, who made more sense for them to protect than their boss?

Something I vowed to keep in mind. Maybe David and I would have to look into just what Director Buckminster himself had been doing that morning...

8

———————

Curious as I was about Secret Service Director Buckminster's day, David and I weren't ready to leave the White House just yet. Or even to come upstairs.

No, we still had to interview those six junior members of the Chief Usher's staff who'd been working that morning.

Poor bastards.

See, in some ways, the investigative training David and I had was kind of similar to the training that police detectives and FBI agents got.

We're both expected to start with very little data, and work to find more, piecing the bigger picture together as we go.

But there's one big, basic difference between all police forces — and I'm including FBI in this — and agents like David and me.

Cops of all stripes have to interview innocent people on a regular basis.

Now, I'm not saying they're good at it, and I'm not saying that plenty of them don't presume guilt or even push for whatever answers they want. There's way too much of that in this country.

But the fact remains that they're trained — or they're *supposed* to be trained — to interview *innocent* people for relevant information. As well as interviewing the guilty.

David and me, and agents like us, we only work with the guilty. Not necessarily criminals, you understand. It's just that, in our line of work — or *old* line of work, I should say — anyone we had to interview this way was already guilty of one thing.

Working against the United States.

Now don't get me wrong. That didn't necessarily mean they'd committed a crime of some sort, or were actively trying to hurt American citizens. Sure, we faced down more than our share of international criminals, but we also dealt with agents of our allies. Who were, every one of them, innately guilty of working against us from time to time.

You see, working for their *own* country meant they weren't working for *our* country.

Which meant that their viewpoint began from, let's just say, an innately adversarial perspective. Because even if those people worked for the United States' allies, their first loyalty was, and had to be, to their own countries.

Common goals sometimes, maybe, but ultimately working from a baseline that could leave us at unexpectedly crossed purposes in the middle of an operation.

Like, say, in the cargo area of a C-130 flying over the Atlantic Ocean in the dead of a winter night. But you didn't hear that from me.

The point is, agents like David and me, we were trained to assume we were *always* at crossed purposes with whoever we interviewed, regardless of who they worked for, or what the circumstances.

Training like that, it has effects you don't think about, when interviewing someone. It affects the way you move. They way you hold yourself. They way phrase things. The way your words come off your tongue.

When dealing with criminals, it tells them not to mess with you.

When dealing with other agents, it tells them you're a pro.

But when dealing with innocent civilians, it seems to tell them that you're judge, jury and executioner and that you're going to pass sentence on them any moment now.

That's my best guess anyway.

Because it *absolutely* ratchets their anxiety levels from would-benefit-from-a-drink-to-soothe-the-nerves all the way to extra-strength-Zoloft-wouldn't-scratch-the-surface.

And beyond.

So no matter how much David and I tried to soothe those poor bastards, our efforts hardly made a dent. We were just too habitually deadly.

And that we were conducting these interviews in a small, white, concrete room that smelled like dust and decay and had a couple of very suspicious brown stains on the floor?

Forget it.

We spent half our interview time with those six poor civilians just calming them enough to get them to a point near coherency.

In short, we didn't get much information from *them*, either. For exactly the opposite reason as from the Secret Service guys. The staffers burbled and panicked and talked nonstop in scattered recollections that included way more than we needed to know about, say, the right way to prepare cuts of New York strip for President Martin's preferred Sunday dinner, or the sixteen reasons that a dust mop was less effective on some kinds of hardwoods than a good, stiff broom, or the eleven tricks to cleaning White House toilets under the rims and lids so that they sparkled enough to be worth saluting.

Problem was, the staffers also jumped around enough in their babbling that it was impossible to tell if they were avoiding saying something they felt guilty about, or if they were sincerely trying to tell us everything they could think of that even *might* have been relevant.

They were just all so scared. Any one of them could've been guilty. Or all of them. Or none of them.

And they were all just worried *sick* about Whiskers. Every one of them had a story to tell about how sweet the little kitten was to them. About how he made a moment for each of them every day, how he perked up when he saw them. How they'd find moments to pet him and play with him, or maybe sneak him a little treat.

Talking about Whiskers, though, was a double-edged sword. It would calm them for a moment, even get them smiling, then they'd remember he was gone and they were off again about some other bit of trivia they'd just remembered.

By the time David and I were done with those interviews, we hadn't established much.

We knew that every one of those staffers loved that cat. I've seen people fake interest in other people's pets, and the concern I was seeing wasn't faked. Whiskers had charmed them, and all six were worried about him.

Interesting that Whiskers didn't seem to have charmed any of the Secret Service agents. Then again, maybe they were just too boring for him to bother with. Too busy being stoic.

Well, all right. Too busy being *on guard*. I might've been angry with them, but they deserved their due. Assuming they were innocent.

Getting back to the staffers, I couldn't be sure they *were* innocent. They were upset about Whiskers, yes, and they were afraid for him. But the problem was, I kept getting this vibe, like maybe they were afraid they were somehow responsible for his catnapping.

The bitch about that was that innocent people sometimes took on guilt that wasn't theirs.

Example. Kid has a bike. Loves his bike. Rides it everywhere, and puts it away in the backyard when he gets home.

One day, kid gets home in a desperate hurry to get to the bathroom. Leaves the bike in his driveway. Just for a minute.

Someone steals the bike.

Kid blames himself, for not putting the bike away. Even though he'd been seconds from an embarrassing accident at the time, and every moment counted.

Kid's parents might even blame him. Saying he didn't take proper care of his bike. Even though they wouldn't have been happy had the kid wet his pants, either.

But the truth is, the theft of the bike is *not the kid's fault.*

There'd been no rash of bike thefts on his block. No posted signs about missing bikes. He had no reason to think he couldn't leave his bike in his own driveway for a few moments, while he relieved himself.

Someone stole that bike. That person, and *that person alone*, is at fault.

Victim blaming drives me crazy.

Unfortunately, it's part of our society. Which meant that one of these frightened staffers might've done something innocuous like leaving a window open while they dusted. And if so, now they're terrified that their little innocuous act led to the catnapping. And that they'll get blamed. Get punished as an accomplice, maybe, or whatever other word they're using on cop shows these days. Accessory, perhaps.

So one of them probably knew something. Even if they didn't know they knew it.

Which meant David and I couldn't let *them* go either.

But it also meant we didn't have our answers yet.

9

With the interviews over, for now at least, David and I moved on to the next most likely source of useful information.

The video feeds.

My personal treat for surviving the interview portion of the day.

Oh sure, I know. Most investigators would rather perform their own root canals than scroll through video recordings, looking for that momentary flash of something interesting.

Me, I liked it. It was kind of a power trip.

You could learn a lot, watching people on video. Even when they knew they were being recorded, there would still be movements they didn't think about. Habits came through. Gestures. For example, almost anyone who was hiding something on their person would have the kind of tell I'd been trained to spot.

And every once in a while, you got a real winner. Somebody so comfortable in their position that they did something goofy because they forgot someone was watching.

I remember going over embassy footage back in ... well, better that I don't say when or where this happened. Point is, the ambassador in question was one of the stiff, formal types. The kind who could starch a napkin by touching it, you know?

Well, after a particularly long day of paperwork in his office — during which I'd witnessed him meeting with the three people he'd admitted to, as well as taking one personal call he'd "forgotten" to mention — he threw some report down on his desk and broke into "Welcome to the Jungle."

I kid you not. This guy who looked like he could kill an informal thought at ten paces with merely a glance. Belted out Axl Rose's lyrics at the top of his lungs. A capella.

While his hands mimed the guitar parts he heard only in his head.

I showed that footage to every agent we had in country. We started privately referring to him as Ambassador Rose.

Oh, he turned out not to be directly guilty of anything. But he *was* connected to someone who was, it turned out. On that private call he hadn't mentioned. Turned out that on the other end of the line was someone who could take otherwise innocuous information from the ambassador and line it up with other sources to cause real problems.

In this case, though, he didn't know what his "friend" was doing. So we didn't come down on him for not putting his bike in the garage. But we made it clear that he needed to prioritize getting to the toilet *before* it became an emergency, if you take my meaning.

That day at the White House, there was no doubt that everyone I'd see on video *had* to know they were being recorded. Every entrance and exit of the White House had a couple of obvious cameras pointed at it.

There were no security cameras *inside* the White House, of course. There were *some* recording devices, but they were strictly for use in record-keeping. Recordings of presidential phone calls, for example, for purposes of transcription and historical records.

But no way anyone, even our allies, would agree to have private meetings with our administration within view of security cameras. To say nothing of the fuss that visiting senators and representatives would kick up.

Unfortunate, in this case. Because I devoutly wished we'd had some kind of camera running in the press room that day. David and I had been through parts of the White House, hoping to find, say, a spot with more than expected cat hair. Enough to indicate serious stress.

See, some cats shed more under stress. I had a big orange tom once who visibly shed during every trip to the vet. Poor little guy. Fortunately his coat was thick enough he didn't develop a bald spot or anything.

Have to say, though, my refusal to put him through that much stress was what led to me finding a vet that made at-home visits. Cost a little more, but it was *so* much easier on my cats.

Anyway, I'd been hoping we'd find some sign of distress from Whiskers that would indicate where he'd been when he'd been catnapped.

Unfortunately, the cleaning staff worked every bit as hard as the chief usher had indicated. We had trouble finding any cat hair *at all*, let alone any beyond normal expectations.

Nevertheless, my gut said that Whiskers had been in the press room when someone snatched him. When those dark blue curtains stood open, it was like a solid wall of windows, looking out over the lawn.

Just the kind of place a small cat might love to go for sunbeams and bird-watching. Plus, Ms. Mackintosh said that the cat wasn't allowed in there.

And anyone who knows anything about cats knows that denying them access to someplace just makes them more fervent to get there.

The White House had been largely empty at the time. None of the normal people were around to stop him. And it had been somewhere close to noon, ensuring that the room should have seen plenty of sun.

The most natural place for a young cat to go would be that press room.

Alas, though, no security footage *inside* the White House. Not even in the press room.

But at least we had a good setup to review what footage there was.

The White House security feeds — what there was of them, anyway — all came to the same room, in the White House basement.

Not to be confused with the subbasements. So this was above the bunkers, a whole passel of situation rooms of all stripes and sizes, and other miscellany, but below the main floors where all — or most — of the politicking happened. The White House basement level had things like the wine cellar, extra food storage, an armory, and all kinds of security offices. Including the video room.

The video room felt like a breath of fresh air, after that interview room with its stains. In here, there was drywall painted a soothing pale blue color. Well, what you could see of the drywall. Because one wall was covered in thirty-inch monitors, and the other three were largely covered in ratty old logs, regulations, procedures, policies, and one absolutely *pristine* series of calendars featuring images and artwork from *Game of Thrones*.

Personally, I couldn't decide if the calendars were out of place or a little too on the nose for D.C.

Worst part? Whole room smelled like burnt coffee. Which, after that *amazing* coffee in the conference room — excuse me, *situation room* — just felt both criminal and a betrayal to the lingering taste of wonderment on my tongue.

Best part? David and I finally got a meal, while we went over the footage. Nothing fancy, but the cheeseburger and fries weren't no drive thru food. These were made personally by the White House chef.

Wagyu burgers, seasoned to perfection and grilled to a magnificent medium rare. And I didn't know where the cheddar cheese came from, but it was so good I wanted to find out and kiss the cows responsible. Lettuce so crisp it might've been picked and washed just in time to be placed on the burger. A scattering of delightfully crunchy and tangy pickles.

The bun was even lightly toasted. Which until that moment I'd never known was how *all burger buns should be served*.

The only side dish was the only one necessary. Fries, salted *just so,* and cooked up crispy enough to give a satisfying crunch, and yet maintained enough heft to be worth chewing.

Now, really, the best thing to go with this meal would've been a beer. Maybe a good Hef, or an IPA. Instead, we were given a choice of sodas.

The message there was clear. No drinking on the job. The chef wanted us to find Whiskers as badly as everyone else did.

Well, we were doing what we could.

The video feeds came in two varieties. There was the outer layer — the cameras covering the area around the entrances and exits to the White House grounds — and the inner layer — the entrances and exits of the White House itself.

We ran them all in sync, one set, and then the other, starting at around ten in the morning — just to pick a time — and continuing until after one.

Every entrance and exit we witnessed on those recordings, and there weren't many of either, matched exactly what we found in the logs.

Except one.

10

At exactly eleven forty-three a.m. Eastern Standard Time, a gardener exited a maintenance gate carrying what appeared to be a sack of leaves.

Outfit looked right, for one of the White House gardeners. Sack looked believable. And raking leaves was a normal Sunday activity, according to the White House Chief Usher's logs.

I could completely understand why no one had noticed that gardener before us.

But there were two definite reasons that gardener with his or her or their "sack of leaves" got our attention.

First, while that gardener *left* with a sack of leaves, that gardener also failed to *return*. With or without a sack of leaves. And no member of the Chief Usher's staff — which to my initial surprise, did include landscaping — was listed in the logs as leaving the grounds within a half hour of that time. Even temporarily. Much less without returning.

Second, and just as important, was that although raking the leaves was a *normal* task for the landscapers on a Sunday morning, no member of the six-person skeleton crew had been assigned to do it that day.

No question. We'd found our catnapper. And now, getting sight of the perp was pumping fire through my system with the need to find this person, make them pay, and get that cat back to his beloved family.

That "sack of leaves" itself looked suspect. It was bulky enough that a soft-sided cat carrier could've been concealed inside it. Which might explain why it wasn't noticeably showing signs of, say, an angry cat trying like heck to get out.

Drugging, of course, was also a possibility. But unless the person was a veterinarian they'd need an accomplice to pull it off. And I mean with a syringe. Say nothing of a stranger trying to *pill* a cat.

Trust me. The White House might've been largely empty that morning, but if some stranger had tried to *pill* Whiskers, *everyone* on the grounds would've known about it. The yowling. The clawing. The spitting.

Forget about it.

Still, the syringe was a possibility. Again, not easy for a layman to pull off, unless they didn't care about *hurting* Whiskers in the process. And I didn't think that hurting the cat was the goal here. Otherwise, there was no need to take him. No, the cat was taken, and for a very specific reason.

Right now, the expectation was ransom of some sort. But something about that felt off. Hours had passed since the catnapping. The catnapper had to know that their deed had been discovered. And yet, no demands were forthcoming.

Which made me worry that this might be a revenge catnapping.

All the more reason to solve it quickly.

"Okay," I said, turning to David. "There's no way this catnapper didn't have some inside help. We're agreed on this?"

He gave me a grim nod.

"That catnapper's heading for a vehicle. One of us needs to see if any sign of that vehicle shows up on anywhere on our footage. Something we can trace. And maybe see if he can find footage of the catnapper entering the grounds. Maybe a face shot. Something."

"That's me," David said, giving me a quick look-over. "You're too angry for video work. Go ask the question we need to ask. Look 'em in that eye and let 'em see you. *Make* 'em answer."

"On it," I said, marching straight out of the video room, past Buckminster — ignoring whatever he asked me as I passed — and straight down to the subbasement where the Twelve Angry Men and Six Frightened Staffers were being held. Each in a separate small, uncomfortable room.

I wouldn't have them brought to me in that interview room. No. I'd go to each of them in turn and say the same thing, starting with the Secret Service agents and working my way through the staffers. And if one of them didn't tell me what I wanted to know, I'd start over. And maybe I wouldn't be so nice about it the second time.

What I said to each of them was this:

"We have video of the catnapper. They're as good as caught. It's just a matter of time. If you had anything to do with this, we *will* find out. And it will go a whole lot better for you if you talk to me *right now*." I paused there, just long enough for my words to sink in, before finishing with, "Do you have anything to tell me?"

Same question put to each of the Twelve Angry Men got me nothing but twelve angry denials and proclamations of their patriotism and integrity.

Same question put to each of the Six Frightened Staffers got me panicked blubbering, tears, denials, and nonsense.

From *five* of them.

The sixth and final one, a tanned man of about thirty years who worked in landscaping and went by the name of James Flaherty, dropped his head and said, "I never dreamed she'd even *touch* that cat."

Bingo.

The problem with this kind of bingo coming at a moment like this one was that I was already so keyed up that I desperately wanted to grab Flaherty and pull the answers right out of his body with my bare hands.

Not the way I needed to go here.

The small, uncomfortable room had a stiff looking couch —

likely a sofa bed — a small coffee table, a small fridge, and two wooden chairs. I could still smell his dinner — fish sticks with too much tartar sauce. Flaherty sat on the couch. On the coffee table was an open bottle of bubbly water, but not the fancy kind.

I grabbed a chair, spun it around and sat with my arms over the back. And well away from the temptation of my weapons.

"The clock is ticking," I said. "And—"

"She'd never kill a cat. I know that. Doesn't have it in her."

Weak reassurance from the man who probably didn't think she had it in her to snatch a cat, either.

"Who are we talking about? Give me a name."

"My cousin. Well, my mom's cousin, technically. I forget what that makes her to me. A cousin once removed, or—"

"*Name.*"

"Colleen Marybeth O'Toole Spinelli."

Quite a name.

"How and why did you help Cousin Colleen today? And what did you *think* she was going to do?"

"I left a window open for her. Just a skosh. Not enough for anyone to notice. She went with President Martin, you see. Well, he wasn't the president then, of course. This was back when they were in college. And she said he stole something of hers. A glass paperweight, with the image of the Space Needle carved inside it."

I knew that paperweight. I'd seen it on the president's desk earlier, when David and I had been looking for cat hair.

"Said she bought it when they were in Seattle. Said he'd had it when they broke up and denied holding on to it. But she'd seen it, of course, in pictures. Knew he had it. Wanted it back."

"Why didn't she ask you to take it?"

"Knew there'd be no point. I'm not a thief, sir, whatever you and the saints might think of me."

"But assisting a theft was all right with you?"

"All I did was leave a window open a skosh, sir. Any thieving she did would be on her soul, not mine." He shook his head. "And she stole a lot more than a paperweight. What was she thinking?"

"I'll ask her," I said, voice flat enough to bring his attention back to the room he was in. "Where is she now?"

"Couldn't begin to guess, sir. I called around, this afternoon. Once it was clear what she'd done. But none of the family knew anything about this. And none of them can get a hold of her. Say her phone only goes to voicemail."

"You didn't call her yourself?"

"Didn't have her number. Never had a reason to call her before, have I? This was something we arranged in person, at the big Flaherty gathering last month."

"I'm glad you see it that way," I said, standing up.

He looked up at me, the portrait of confusion.

"That it was something *you both* arranged," I clarified.

"Not *this*, sir," he said quickly. "Never this. I love that cat like he was my own. I could *kill* Colleen for stealing him. And if she harmed a hair on his blessed little head, I just may."

"The degree of your guilt will be for the Justice Department to decide," I said. "Right now, though, if you know *anything* else that might help me, you'd better tell me before I open this door."

"She didn't take a plane, sir. I know that. She lives in Chicago, but when she moved there from Boston, she drove out, rather than sedate her Danny Boy for the flight."

"Wait," I said, frowning. "She's had cats of her own?"

"Long as I've been alive, she has, sir. Though come to think of it, she was still mourning Danny Boy at the gathering."

"When did Danny Boy pass?"

"Last winter, sir."

And pieces began to fall into place.

11

I RAN ALL THE WAY FROM FLAHERTY'S LITTLE NOT-OFFICIALLY-A-CELL TO the video room.

David was scrolling the feeds on every one of those thirty-inch monitors, displaying shots near the maintenance gate at two different times. Both of them seemed to feature the same small black SUV.

I snatched one of his forgotten fries as I dropped back into the seat beside him.

"I've got a name," I said. "Colleen Marybeth O'Toole Spinelli."

"That's a lot of name," he said, voice absent. He was clicking a mouse button and sending some still shots to a printer in the corner, which complained, but hummed to life and started slowly committing the chosen images to paper.

"She's mother's cousin to one James Flaherty."

"Gardener," David said, voice still absent. "Tall. Tanned. Slight hitch in his step from an old injury to his right ankle. Build displays admirable upper-body strength, but no scars, and no indication from his knuckles that he's a brawler."

"That's the guy," I said. "And good eye. I'd missed that about the knuckles. Anyway, he left a window open for her so she could steal back a paperweight from the president's desk that she claimed to have bought in Seattle."

David frowned and turned to me. "Space Needle?"

I nodded.

"She didn't take it."

"No, she took Whiskers instead."

"And she left in this SUV," he said, nodding at the screen. "Can you make out that license plate number? I can't get past the first couple of characters."

I stared at three different fuzzy images. Willing them to come further into focus.

Didn't actually work, of course, but zeroing in with my complete attention that way did help. Along with a simple, centering exercise that controlled my breathing.

"Three ... Sierra ... Tango ... eight..."

"Roger on the Three Sierra Tango. But you're sure that's an eight? Looks like it might be Bravo."

"Definitely an eight," I said. "You can just make out the little dent on the left side of it."

David shook his head. "Maybe *you* can. My contacts may need a new prescription."

"The next one..." I said, biting my lip now. "I *think* the next character is Oscar."

"Not Delta?"

I stared a moment longer. Desperately trying to see if the left side of that character had telltale rounding at the top and bottom...

"Oscar. Definitely." I shook my head, and rubbed my eyes as I turned back to him. "Can't make out the rest. Angle and clarity suck."

"Yes they do," he said. "But that'll have to be enough to go on." He sighed. "What do you think?"

I knew what he was asking. With that much information, the right people wouldn't need long to get the rest of that plate number and put out an APB on the vehicle. Find it in a matter of hours.

But this process would also get *way* too many people involved, considering it was supposed to be done as quietly as possible.

"Can't get loud about this," I said with a sigh.

"Don't see that we have a choice. She's had time to board a plane."

"Flaherty says she won't fly with a cat. Won't sedate him."

"Boat then? Train?"

"No," I said. "Too risky. Either of those would put her too close to too many people, and that cat's just too recognizable. If she won't sedate a cat to fly, she won't do it to hide herself. That means she's still in that SUV. We just have to find her."

"Flaherty know where she lives?"

"Chicago. But she'd be an idiot to go there."

"Everyone's an idiot sometimes," David said. "Hell, you were playing *soccer* this morning."

"Bite your tongue. Soccer's practically a religion in Portland. And I don't think Chicago's right."

"Why not?"

"Flaherty was calling around to family, trying to find her. Phone's straight to voicemail, which suggests she might not even have it on her."

"So we couldn't use it to track her."

"Yep. And what would your family do if you were the catnapper and they couldn't get you on the phone?"

"Come to my house," David said with a sigh. "Might be the only way to get my parents to visit."

"So she won't want to be there when they arrive."

David gave me a look of realization.

"Could be a second reason to ditch the phone. I know I can think of one that might have occurred to her, when she planned this."

I frowned as I thought about that. Then it clicked.

"It would be useless anyway, if she didn't pay for *an international plan*."

David nodded. "She's heading for Canada. Got to be."

"The border's ... what? Eight hours from here?"

"Closer to nine. Maybe more. Stops for food, gas, bathroom. Plus, she won't want to risk getting pulled over so she'll be rock solid on that speed limit the whole way. Maybe even under it a tad, for safety."

"Still doesn't give us much time. She's got a lead on us of more than" — I glanced at my smartwatch — "seven hours. Maybe as many as eight."

"No time to waste."

We were up and out of our chairs then, and running as soon as David grabbed his printouts.

This time Buckminster wouldn't let me get by him. Little bastard ran right alongside us like he went running in a suit every day.

"What do you have?"

"Wasn't any of your people," I said.

"I knew that."

"The rest is—"

"Wait," Buckminster said, grabbing me by the lapel of my gray suit and pulling us to a stop.

David had his knife drawn and ready, held down where the director couldn't see. Even with his dancing eyes.

I looked at the hand on my lapel and then met Buckminster's eyes. And the look I gave him was not friendly.

"Are you interfering with our investigation, Director Buckminster?"

"No, dammit," he said, "but you *will* listen to me."

I looked at the hand still on my lapel.

He released it. I smoothed my suit. "Talk then. We're in a hurry."

"Let my people help."

"This is our task."

"And you're in charge of it. No question. But right now you're in a hurry, yes? And you need resources, don't you."

David slipped that knife back into his wrist sheath and shot his cuffs.

"Look," Buckminster said, talking to both of us now as David stepped back into easy view. "My people failed today. They know it. The whole damned White House knows it. And I know this is your task. I'm not trying to get them any credit for it."

"It's not about—" I started, but David cut me off.

"Let him finish, Hank."

I nodded for Buckminster to continue.

"The president needs confidence in his Secret Service. He relies on us every single day, to protect both him and his family. If this failure hangs over us, it will undercut his confidence, and may cause him distraction at a dangerous moment. May make him question decisions and courses of action that he should be able to take with perfect certainty."

I doubted President Martin *ever* had the luxury of perfect certainty. But I didn't see any point in saying so.

"Right now, I've got twelve men who would *kill* to make up for today's lapse."

"We don't need them to kill," I said.

"I meant that figuratively. Certainly more figuratively than your colleague here meant by drawing a knife on me."

David didn't bother hiding his surprise, and neither did I. I was positive that David's movements had never been in the director's sightlines. As, apparently, was David.

"Please," Buckminster said. "I rose to this position for a reason. I knew where the knife was, and there was only one reason to keep it out of my sight when you felt under threat." He straightened his own lapels. "But I see no reason to make an issue of that lapse in judgment. After all, anyone can make a mistake, not so? And should be given the opportunity to prevent that mistake from expanding into a bigger problem?"

"We are pressed for time," David said softly.

I nodded. "All right. We've got a name, partial plate, partial shots of the SUV she's driving, and a reasonably certain destination."

Buckminster's eyebrows went up. "Impressive. Where's she headed?"

"Canada," I said. "And with her lead, she might reach the border inside two hours."

"We may need to bring in Homeland Security," David said. "Have her detained at the border. But we've got to insist neither she nor the vehicle are searched."

"Forget it," Buckminster scoffed. "Bring in Homeland Security on anything with need-to-know information and they won't leave it to the border patrol. They'll bring in their bulldog division, and both she and that cat might get shot in an 'unfortunate misunderstanding.'"

"I hate it," I said, "but I don't see where we have a choice. We'll never catch her in time."

Buckminster chuckled. "You forget, Agent Sauer, that the Secret Service is part of the *Treasury* Department." He winked at me. "I think we can find it in our budget to pay for a little extra speed in a situation like this one."

12

———————

Buckminster wasn't kidding about speed. Soon as we started hustling up the concrete hall, he got on his phone while keeping pace.

By the time the three of us, plus the Twelve Angry Men, got out of our respective basement and subbasement locations and reached the White House helipad — and understand, we were *running* the whole way — he had a freaking *Lockheed-Martin VH-92A helicopter* waiting for us, spun up and ready to fly.

I developed a new respect for Director Buckminster the moment I saw that copter. Same make and model as *Marine One* — not the same copter of course — and he just pulls it out of his pocket like he's going to ask, "Is *this* your card?"

Sent a chill right through me that said I should never, ever mess with this man.

The copter whisked us through the muggy, late afternoon sky to the airport so fast I didn't have time to wonder which airport we were landing at.

Actually, I'm not sure of that. It's entirely possible that I'd figured out exactly which local airport we'd gotten to in record time. I might even have noticed how fast we were flying, or gotten the name of our pilot, a cheerful young woman who seemed certain she was doing something exciting.

I might possibly have known all of those things.

But seeing the plane waiting for us on that tarmac, all fueled up and ready to go, drove every one of those thoughts right out of my head and made me turn to stare slack-jawed at the magician known as Secret Service Director Buckminster.

"You got us a freaking *Concord*?" I had to shout over the rotors and vibrations of the helicopter, but honestly I might've shouted it anyway.

I did, at least, have the self-control not to say anything into the mic, where the pilot would hear us.

"What?" he shouted, grinning at me. "Think Miles would want me pinching pennies while his cat gets a Canadian driver's license?"

We hustled out of the helicopter, across the hot, oily-smelling tarmac, and up the stairs into the belly of the Concord. We were barely strapped in before it started moving.

This wasn't just any Concord, either. I mean, I always thought of this design as the perfect plane for the impatient rich. The kind of people who'd *just have* to "breakfast" in France and "dinner" in ... I don't know ... Japan.

But the interior of this particular Concord was spartan. Simple, pale gray and dark blue color scheme. Twenty seats designed for efficiency, rather than comfort. Minimal padding. And they faced each other across the narrow belly of the plane. There was cargo netting front and back. And yeah, I could see a sign indicating a restroom, but given everything else I was seeing, I didn't figure it would be more than a bucket-sized chemical toilet and a tube of hand sanitizer.

David and I sat on one side, with five of the Secret Service agents around us. Director Buckminster sat directly opposite me, with the other agents arrayed around him.

David chuckled. Nudged me in the ribs. "Slowest plane we've flown today, huh?"

Damn it, now he had me chuckling too. "Most comfortable, too."

"And a better soundtrack."

"You didn't like the music?"

"I prefer country and western," David said. "You know. Real music. *Storytelling* music."

"Rock and metal tell stories too."

"Sure. Sure. About drugs, maybe. Or sex. Or—"

"Hate to break up such scintillating conversation," Buckminster said, and I realized he didn't have to say it very loud for us all to hear.

The main part of this Concord was so simple I'd been thinking of it as a military plane. And military planes can be noisy as hell. But this one wasn't much louder than, say, a commercial 737.

"We'll be there in less than an hour," he continued. "Maybe we should talk about how this is going to work?"

"Sure," I said, then got a sinking feeling in my stomach. I couldn't think of any especially convenient airports to Peace Bridge, which was what David and I figured had to be the perp's choice of crossing points. "Where will we be setting down?"

Buckminster laughed, and a few of his agents laughed along with him.

"We're not landing," he said. "We're not going to have time to get clearance at an airport, touch down, deplane, board a vehicle—"

"You don't mean..." I said, as that sinking feeling started telling me *I told you so.*

"Yep," he said with a smile and a nod. "We'll have to parachute in."

"Better use Front Park as our landing zone then," I said. "Biggest patch of green close to Peace Bridge and the border."

"We better call ahead and warn them," David said.

"On it," Buckminster said, turning to the two men closest to his right. "Get it done, Jefferson. Madison, you update the pilot."

Jefferson nodded, took out his phone, and went to work, while Madison unstrapped and strode purposefully toward the cockpit.

David leaned in close. "I haven't jumped in at least twenty years."

"Me either," I lied. "Got a better idea?"

"Better? Many. That will get us there in time? No."

"Right," I said, louder. "We 'chute in to Front Park. On a Sunday evening, traffic should be slow with vacationers going back across the border both directions."

"Problem there," David said, "is that the route to the bridge is a freeway. No convenient stoplights."

"But it *is* a toll bridge," I said. "And only three lanes total, both directions. Center lane can go either way, depending on what they need. So worst case scenario, two lanes going Canada-ward, both slowed down by the toll, and the stop at customs on the far side."

"Plus the slowdown of any traffic. Which there most likely will be."

"Too risky," Buckminster said. "We wait until she's on the bridge and we *miss*, she's across the border and we can't touch her. Not without going through channels and making a *lot* of noise."

"I agree," I said, surprising him. "Plus, if we wait until she's on the bridge, we'll end up stopping *all* traffic. Which will require explanations to our own border people, as well as our northern friends. I just wanted to establish the situation, so it's clear to all of us."

"Fair enough," Buckminster said with a nod. "Now what's the plan?"

"That depends, can you get us two vehicles? Bulky by preference?"

"Two? Where we're going?" Buckminster shook his head. "Maybe, but I doubt it. I can get us one, for sure. In Washington I could get two with a phone call, here it's a favor to even get one. I know who to call to make the border guys—"

"Not the border guys," I said quickly. "We need to avoid them. I was thinking of the Public Bridge Authority. Local guys, not feds. Maybe a little easier for your title to push around."

"Definitely easier *and* quieter," Buckminster said, approving. "But no guarantee they'll have what we need."

"Get the best we can."

"Tell me the rest, first."

"After we 'chute in, we split up. There are two ninety-degree bends in the road leading to the final approach to the bridge. Both work to our advantage, and both of them just off that park. A right turn around the end of it, then a left turn that will pass the wide open area of the Bridge Authority. That's where we need to take her down."

David nodded. "Two two-man teams of spotters at the corners, plus one more, say, by the freeway at the southern end of the park?"

I nodded. "And one more team of four at the toll plaza, in case of the worst. Last ditch effort, if the main plan fails. The takedown team will consist of you, me, Director Buckminster, and two agents of your choice, director."

"Hamilton and Adams," Buckminster said smoothly. "What about the vehicles?"

"We find out when exactly she's coming, and how fast, so we can time our move. We roll out of the massive parking lot and block the road in front of her. Make the arrest. Quick and quiet as possible, then let the tourists get back to their crossing."

"Not too quiet," David said. "We need to flash badges during the takedown."

"Right," I said in sudden understanding. "Witnesses are inevitable, and they'll need to see that this is a government thing, not a kidnapping or some kind of O.C. move. Good thinking, David."

Crap. I *was* retired if I missed that one.

"Right," Buckminster said, pulling out his phone. "I'll see what I can do for vehicles."

13

———————

I tell everyone that I hate to skydive.

Totally a lie though. I freaking love it.

But I *tell* everyone that I hate it because I love it a little *too* much, you know? The *rush* you get when you're falling from a great height, staring death in the face...

...then thumbing your nose at him by pulling the rip cord.

There's just nothing like it.

I like it so much I worry it could become an addiction. And then I'd end up doing it too often. Especially if I started hanging out with other skydivers. Enablers, if you will. I might find myself taking a stupid risk, so I don't miss out on the rush.

Like jumping when I hadn't had enough sleep. Or maybe when one of my old injuries was acting up.

I mean, I could seriously hurt myself if I tried skydiving when my ankle was locked up. But if I got into the habit of jumping on a regular basis, well, I might have a moment of madness or idiocy and end my life a *little* too quickly.

Too quickly *for me*, anyway. I'm sure there are plenty of people who firmly believe I've lived too long as it is.

And even if I survived an ill-chosen jump, I might maim my leg beyond my ability to use it in my daily life.

So I only rarely go skydiving, recreationally. Never more than once a season. I require myself to leave the state to do it, and I don't let myself jump in the same state twice in a row. Just little roadblocks to slow me down. Dampen my enthusiasm.

But this, today, this wasn't recreational. This was a job requirement. I had to do this. For my country. And for Whiskers.

So it was all I could do to keep the silly grin off my face as I checked my chute and backup to make sure they were packed right, then strapped the pack on like I was settling into a favorite chair.

Must've had that telltale gleam in my eye, though, because as we were lining up to jump from the gray interior of the Concord out into the twilight sky, Director Buckminster shook his head at me.

"How the hell do *you* survive retirement?" he asked.

"He changed religions," David said. "He's an acolyte of the Church of Association Football now."

That got a good laugh all around, but from the look in David's eye, I suspected he had questions for me later.

Obviously we didn't try to make our jump while flying at Mach speeds. I mean, there's stupid and there's *stupid*, you know?

The pilot wasn't flying due north at that point anyway. That would've taken us into Canadian airspace and raised an unfortunate number of questions.

But a private jet veering *just inside* Canadian airspace while visibly turning about because "they realized their mistake," well, that was hardly an incident worth raising.

So our pilot — whom I never met, by the way. One Secret Service agent or another handled all interactions with the cockpit — had been on a slow bend west on our way toward south-by-southwest and so forth until he or she could eventually take the plane back ... wherever it came from.

Which meant we were flying at a reasonable speed and height when the time came for us to jump into the night air.

My nerves were already dancing the salsa before the all-clear came. I had that good, good tension in my belly and muscles. Eager to hit the sky.

I'd be jumping first. Then Buckminster. Then the Secret Service agents. David would jump last. We'd gather in the air according to our teams, and aim our landings appropriately.

I got to open the door. This plane was actually equipped with a sliding door, as though we would not be the first people using it for parachuting.

A Concord. With a parachute door.

That raised all kinds of questions in my head, but I had the feeling that the answers would not be forthcoming from Buckminster.

The whipping wind smelled sweet. Like a brisk, chilled white wine after coming inside on a hot day. The feel of it on my face was a blessing.

See, that was part of what I hated about Air Force Four-and-a-Half. If my skin was going to get rippled, I preferred it to be done by the sky itself. Preferably while I'm falling a long distance, with a good chute on my back.

The call came over the intercom. "In position. Jump when ready."

I took my last step forward. As I did, Buckminster slapped me on the back and said, "Good luck."

That slap messed up my stride. Sole of my loafer — yes, I was jumping in a gray suit and loafers. Though I did, at least, have goggles on — caught the edge of the fuselage and twisted my foot the wrong way.

My left ankle immediately locked in a bent position. Muscles clamping down in painful seizure.

I didn't so much jump out of the plane as slip and fall.

The good side?

I was now skydiving. That part I loved. It doesn't feel so much like falling, to me at least, as it does like being held up by the wind. But the wind is porous, so you feel like you're slowly sliding toward the ground.

That's a lie, of course. I was actually plummeting at speeds that rapidly approached terminal velocity. But that was what it felt like to me, and I gave myself a moment to indulge in the fantasy of not just flying, but of being held up by the wind itself. Like the hand of some sky goddess caressing me. Refusing to let death have me, because I was special.

Normally I could indulge in that feeling for the better part of thirty, maybe even forty-five seconds depending on the jump.

From the height we were jumping, I should've had maybe twenty, twenty-five seconds to enjoy it.

But my ankle was screaming at me. So I got maybe ten seconds of fun before reality settled in.

I was going to have to land on one foot.

That had to be the worst idea I'd heard in ages.

Not an exaggeration, though. If I tried to use my left foot in my landing, with my ankle locked, I'd probably break that ankle. I'd be just this side of completely useless, when little Whiskers needed me the most.

But it was my day for madness or idiocy. Because just as I was gathering with my team — David, Buckminster, Hamilton and Adams — I'd thought of a way to land that wouldn't put my ankle to any undue risk. Or even risk hurting my other ankle, which was a distinct possibility, if I tried to land using only the one.

Oh, I'd ruin my suit. But hey, ruining the loaner suit I'd been given for the day was a price I was willing to pay to save my ankles.

Assuming this crazy stunt worked.

"I'll meet up with you," I yelled to the others. Then I steered away from them, by pulling in my limbs in the direction I wanted to go. Which was a little further east — and a little further south — than we'd planned on for my approach. I'd need the space.

I pulled my chute only a two-one-thousand count after the others pulled theirs, but that would buy me about five seconds of actual lead time. Just in case one of us was off in our aim.

I'd hate to get the landing right, only to end up in a position where someone else landed *on* me.

I pulled the ripcord. My chute inflated, yanking me back up like a final caress from that sky goddess. (Over the years, I'd named her Cerellia.) And what some people don't realize, is that you can actually steer a chute, within certain parameters.

And I was steering back north. Fast.

Normally, I liked to land at a little angle, so I could have an easy time hitting the ground moving, and dropping my chute behind me.

This time, I was going forward — north — at two, maybe three times my normal rate. Changing my usual angle of twenty-five, maybe thirty degrees to closer to forty-five...

Now fifty...

Now sixty...

I gritted my teeth as the ankle-breaking ground loomed ever closer. Looked as though our landing zone was a huge soccer field. And whatever arrangements Agent Jefferson had made for us had it lit up like it was game night.

I pushed for yet a steeper angle.

Now sixty-five degrees. I was outside acceptable operating parameters for my chute. I wasn't sure how much more it could take. It was fighting me with everything it had. I strained with every muscle in my arms and shoulders, torso and back — including my abs, yanking my hips and legs up and holding them in position.

I yelled my best battle roar, giving this everything I had.

Seventy-degrees.

"Come on," I growled.

The ground was getting closer faster than I was gaining angle.

The chute gave out first. Released on me when I was maybe ten feet up.

But I'd managed seventy-five degrees.

I hit that grass like I was making a slide tackle on an ambitious forward, with the game on the line.

Pretty sure I would've gotten a yellow card for this one. Because I came in spikes high.

I hit the grass, sliding on my butt and back. Oh, I'd have plenty of bruises from this, that was certain. But I'd avoided breaking anything, at least.

When I finally came to a halt on my long, long slide, I ended up between David and Buckminster.

David threw his arms out to the sides and yelled, "Safe!"

I groaned. "Wrong sport, you idiot!"

But from the laughter in David's eye, he already knew that.

14

My ankle was still locked up. I'd bruised pretty much every part of my back between my hamstrings and shoulders, and tweaked my neck. Come to think of it, my abs and stomach weren't all that happy with me either.

Apparently, I hadn't finished digesting that magnificent burger and fries back at the White House — which explained why I still had a little taste of them lingering in my mouth — and my stomach was now registering formal complaints at all this activity while it was trying to work.

I informed my stomach that its complaints were duly noted, and would be entered into the record.

With that moment of near-internal reckoning forestalled, as soon as David and Buckminster helped me up, I was mobile. After a fashion. Slow and hobbling, but mobile.

"Don't wait for me," I ordered. "I'll catch up."

David, Buckminster, Hamilton and Adams all ran north to the Bridge Authority to meet with whatever contact the director had set up, and get two things done quickly.

First, get someone to drive the toll booth team to their post.

Though from the look of things, that team might beat my team to the Bridge Authority and get their own part started.

What can I say? My team was slowed by my little floor show.

David and I were mic'd up now, on Secret Service radios, to keep us all in the loop.

So while I managed a slow, loping, painful form of limping jog across the kind of lush, full, even lawn I *never* got to play soccer on anymore — which struck me as monumentally unfair, given that I just managed the slide tackle of my life — I was listening on the radio while the different teams called in with updates.

The two corner teams of spotters were first to call in that they were in-position and ready.

I pushed for more speed, and damn how much it hurt. Managed to lope fast enough that I could be considered moving at what would normally be a brisk walk.

I'd pay for it later, of course. My ankle and shin were *loudly* informing me so with every step. But I couldn't let Whiskers down.

The spotters at the southern end called in-position by the time I reached tarmac.

Oddly, the tarmac was slightly less painful for me to move across. Maybe because it was smooth and stable, whereas every step on thick grass meant slight angle changes.

Whatever the reason I pushed harder for speed. Sweating, and gritting against my many discomforts.

Now here's the thing. Right now, some people would look at my situation and say that I was getting too old for this.

I say bullshit.

My problem here was not *age*. My problem here was an old injury to my ankle, which had locked it up. I'd've been facing the same problem if I'd had the same injury at twenty-five or thirty.

Though, admittedly, at those ages it wouldn't have slowed me down *as much* as it did now.

Point is, it was the *injury* that was my problem as I ran across that field of grass and onto the tarmac of the Bridge Authority's oversized parking lot. Not my age. If my ankle hadn't locked up, I would've been leading the pack out there.

Here endeth the lesson.

The twilight sky was purpling its way toward black. The warm summer breeze felt chilly, which told me I was running way too hot.

Couldn't be helped.

By the time I caught up with my team, the toll bridge team had called in-position, and I learned the hard way that my team had acquired...

...one car.

Not even an *SUV*. A *car*.

Not even a *big* car.

A *Prius*.

A white Prius with Buffalo and Port Eerie Public Bridge Authority proudly *emblazoned* on the sides.

To his credit, Director Buckminster looked embarrassed. Even while his eyes seemed once again to be checking every direction at once.

"It's the best they could give us on short notice," he said, holding up the fob.

"It'll do," I said. "Change of plans, though. I can't drive it right now."

"I'm glad *you* said it," David said softly.

"We'll handle the car. Adams, you're behind the wheel. Hamilton, riding shotgun with badge and weapon ready." Buckminster tossed the fob straight into Adams' hands while still looking at me. Despite the fact that Adams stood behind him. "No point having anyone in the back. Too slow to get out."

"I agree. You're with me and David. One of you on driver's door—"

"Me," David said.

"Fine. You're on passenger door, director. I'll go in the back. Whiskers is most likely back there. Behind a seat, maybe." I turned to the two Secret Service agents. "Adams, Hamilton, you're on crowd control once she's stopped. You two jump out and flash badges nice and high and guns down low. Clear?"

"Clear, sir," they said, which surprised me. But then, maybe calling me "sir" was their way of calling me "old man."

Whatever.

The three of us took up position, hiding behind a row of planters at the southwest corner of the parking lot, nearest the road. Me on the outside, because I was slowest. I'd go around. David and the director would go over the planters.

In the Prius, Adams and Hamilton had the engine running — if what that engine did could be called "running." "Humming" maybe — while sitting just back from the exit, pretending to be on their phones.

Traffic was lighter than I expected. I'd hoped for bumper-to-bumper, but expected pretty thick. Back here it was more like a semi or two would come along, causing a little slowdown, but it would pick up once the semis were gone.

Sure, the traffic I was seeing wasn't going more than thirty-five, maybe forty miles per hour, but that was still faster than I liked for this.

The real bridge and customs slowdown wasn't coming for another few hundred feet. Which made me question my choice of action spots. But if we'd tried to move down there, we'd've had no hiding places. We could've risked her spotting us, yanking the wheel left and forcing her way into and across the U.S. Customs side of things.

She might've been gone before we could stop her. With no sense of where she'd try to cross next. As good as gone.

No. this spot was the best I had. I just had to hope—

The call came from the first group of spotters, at the southern end of the park.

"We have visual contact. Black SUV, moving in a pack of cars. License plate Three Sierra Tango eight Delta seven niner. One occupant. Female. Black hair. Western European descent. Approximately forty-five years of age."

"Sounds like our perp," I said into the mic. "Ready everyone."

"Visual contact," someone from the second group said. I didn't know his name, but it was probably Washington or Franklin or Hancock or something like that. "Estimated speed thirty-eight miles per hour. In right-hand lane. Taking the first corner ... now."

"Adams," I said.

Adams pulled up to the curb and put his blinker on.

"Visual contact." That was from the third and closest set of spotters. Jefferson on the mic. "Slowing for — Negative! Accelerating! We've been made! She's trying to force her way left."

Damn it! I knew this team was too big.

"Go, go, go!" I shouted into the mic.

I jumped up and hobbled around the side. Making my best time for the freeway. David and Buckminster both vaulted their planters with admirable agility. And Adams...

Well, in Adams' defense, let me just say this.

Since the Prius was first introduced to the market, many versions of that car have been made available. Some of them, I understand, can be downright sporty.

This, however was not *that* kind of Prius.

I didn't know the details of its manufacturing year or the subtleties of its model and options, but I can tell you without fear of contradiction that this particular Prius leapt forward with the grace, speed, and agility of an inebriated slug.

It managed to get into the street, all right. But Spinelli's SUV was already forcing its way into the left-hand lane, and I could see Spinelli looking at the expansive customs parking lot with wide, hopeful eyes.

She'd gone too fast, though. Accelerating the way she did, she lost the cover of her pack of cars. Leaving her momentarily wide open.

David must've seen the same thing I did. Because we both stopped moving and raised our weapons.

Buckminster, unsurprisingly, was already taking aim.

"Tires *only!*" I barked.

All three of us opened fire. Each of us knowing full well he'd only get one shot.

I was shaky. Hot. Hurting. Covered in sweat.

But no way was I letting that cat down.

I hit the SUV's front right tire.

David hit the rear right.

Buckminster, far as I could tell, only hit the tarmac. Though his shot might've ricocheted into the underside of the vehicle. I don't know.

And Colleen Marybeth O'Toole Spinelli might have been many things, but a stunt driver she was *not*.

She immediately struggled for control, while Adams finally got the Prius in front of her.

David and Buckminster were both waving credentials and yelling for traffic to stop while I was trying to catch up to them.

But we did our jobs.

David yanked the perp out of the driver's seat, while Buckminster covered him from the other door.

I ripped open the back door.

Belted into the back seat was a small, tan, soft-sided cat carrier.

Inside that cat carrier, yowling complaints — with a surprisingly strong voice, given how long he'd likely been complaining — was Whiskers.

I wanted to get him out of that carrier. Take him in my arms and hold him. But he was too panicked. He'd bolt. So I settled for lifting him up — in the carrier — to where we could see each other.

"It's okay, little guy," I said to him in the gentle tones I use when addressing all cats for the first time. "You're safe now. We're here to take you home to your family."

I don't know if it was my tone, or if it was the fact that I wasn't Spinelli, or if maybe he smelled the White House on me.

But Whiskers started purring.

15

———

I HAVE TO ADMIT. HAVING SECRET SERVICE DIRECTOR BUCKMINSTER on-site for the final takedown was a big help in the cleanup.

While I thought of the director as the sort of small, nondescript man who could be an extremely successful assassin, when it came to speaking Bureaucrat, the man's command wasn't just fluent, it was *idiomatic.*

And he peppered just enough ring of authority into his voice to smooth over any bureaucratic rough patches.

Though admittedly, his title probably helped.

He fed the locals a line about this woman being wanted for federal crimes of a sensitive nature that were beyond their pay grades, and pretty much left it at that. But he did it in such a way that they were *thanking* us for disrupting traffic and getting their Prius into a fender-bender.

Yeah, apparently while I was busing shooting out a tire, some madman or idiot had tried cutting around the SUV to the left and clipped the Prius. Adams and Hamilton were okay, though.

Soon enough, we were on a flight back to D.C. with Whiskers in tow.

Best part?

I got to be the one opening the soft-shell carrier inside the Yellow Oval Room of the White House. Which meant I got a front row seat to watch Whiskers run right into little Shonda's arms while President Martin and the First Lady beamed at all of us.

Yeah, we got handshakes and hugs and pats on the back and effusive verbal praise and promises of future favors and all like that.

But the best reward I got that day was that moment when Whiskers leaped into Shonda's arms.

There is no smile like the smile of a little girl getting her beloved pet back. I swear. I didn't feel any of my aches and pains for a good half-hour after seeing that smile. Not even the aftermath of my locked ankle (which had relaxed on the flight back to D.C., thank god).

Then, of course, reality set in, and President Martin *insisted* that his personal physician be the one to check me out and tell me that I shouldn't be doing things like this anymore.

It was the "anymore" that irritated me. Truth was, *no one* should have to do things like this. Regardless of their age.

But so long as humans out there will steal cats, or secrets, or commit any number of other crimes, people like me *have* to do "things like this" and stop them.

The exam and x-rays — all clean, at least, so I didn't break anything — took long enough that David was able to return and give me the answer my big lingering question.

Turned out that it hadn't been a *paperweight* Colleen Spinelli née O'Toole accused her then-boyfriend Miles Martin of stealing from her. It had been a tabby cat *named* Paperweight. (Apparently because of his tendency to sprawl on important papers.)

The president assured us both that he'd gotten Paperweight long before he'd ever met Colleen, and that Paperweight had always been *his* cat.

I have to admit, though, I wondered a little about that. Not that President Martin was lying to me. I'd been trained to spot liars, and I was sure the president meant every word.

It's just, that ... well ... cats are living beings, not simple possessions. Yeah, living with a cat can make that cat feel like yours. But the truth is, cats pick their own people.

So maybe Paperweight stayed with then-college-student Miles Martin because he liked Martin better. Or maybe Paperweight would have preferred to leave with Colleen O'Toole when they broke up.

I'd never know the truth there.

But either way, it didn't justify her trying to steal Whiskers, a cat to whom she had *no* claim *whatsoever*. So at the end of the day, I knew I'd done the right thing.

David opted for flying back on Air Force Four-and-a-Half. Apparently he had some kind of date the next day that he didn't want to miss. But before he left, he made a comment about skydiving that made me think we'd have a conversation about it sometime soon. Given that we both lived in Portland, and all.

That could wait, though. And no way was I boarding that little speedball again if I didn't have to. No, I offered to let the president fly me home commercial. Most I'd hoped for was a first class ticket.

The president wouldn't hear of it, though. He chartered a private plane for me, followed by a limo ride back to my house.

And I think President Martin had the plane's flight crew told I was some kind of hero, because they were friendlier and more helpful than on any flight I could ever remember. But maybe that's just the typical charter experience. I wouldn't know.

I stayed awake on the flight, though. Oh, I *could've* slept. I was practically dead on my feet, even without all the bruises.

But I wanted to wait until I could get home so I could fall into bed, surrounded by my own kitties.

Which was what I did.

The minute I came in the front door, Sturm and Drang let me know how upset they were with me for my absence. They were a pair of rescue kitties. Apparently someone had been breeding a Russian Blue, and learned to their dismay that some tabby father had snuck in. Meaning that my little Sturm and Drang weren't "purebred." As though I cared.

They were mischievous and affectionate little blue-gray fuzzballs with darker tabby markings. And they loved me.

So yes, they emphasized their displeasure at my absence by tipping over all the garbage cans in the house. That was true. And they did it while meowing in sharp tones meant to censure me.

But the moment I flopped on my bed, they appeared so fast they might've teleported onto my chest. Nuzzling my face and purring as they demanded their proper due of attention.

And let me tell you. After a long, hard day, that was the best way to fall asleep that I knew of.

EPILOGUE

Traumatic as the Day of Weak Sunbeams had been, Whiskers decided that some good had come out of his little misadventure.

For one thing, everyone was more affectionate. Rumble Laugh, Sweet Voice and Nuzzle all fairly *doted* on him. Even making other two-legs wait while they paid him some attention whenever he came into the room, no matter what they'd been doing at the time.

And they weren't the only ones. All the other members of the pride made more time for Whiskers. Gave him more pets and scritches and treats. Even the rigid two-legs started petting him now and again.

And best of all?

No one chased him out of the Bird Viewing Room anymore. No matter what was going on in there, no matter how many yowly two-legs all thrust their forepaws at Rumble Laugh and yowled for his attention, no one tried to bar Whiskers from coming in ... winding around their legs if he felt like it ... even clawing at the curtains that blocked his view of Outside.

Why, Whiskers had even climbed those curtains while the room was full of yowly two-legs, and no one got mad at him. Some of them even gave happy laughs, including Rumble Laugh himself.

Oh, Rumble Laugh took Whiskers down from the curtain, but he held and petted Whiskers while he dealt with pride matters.

And if no one was in there, and the curtains were open, Whiskers was welcome to go watch the birds and squirrels and lie in the sunbeams all he wanted. Nuzzle would even join him, and no one got mad.

Yes, a lot of good had ended up coming out of that bad, bad day. Which was something Whiskers contemplated once in a while, while he bathed. That good could come out of bad, that was a mystery of Bast that Whiskers could not pretend he understood. Perhaps he was too young, yet.

Still.

For the first several days after he got home, Whiskers didn't like going to sleep when he was alone in a room. Sometimes he'd wake up, and if no one was around, he'd panic and go running and yowling for Nuzzle or Rumble Laugh or Sweet Voice.

And so far, one of them had always answered. Which did a great deal to ease those worries.

And whenever it happened, Whiskers noticed that some of the other two-legs, even sometimes the rigid two-legs, would come reassure him that he was safe and with the pride.

But what eased those worries most, and made them finally go away, was something that he realized during a contemplative bath many days later.

He didn't have to worry.

Yes, it was true, someone might try to steal him away again. It had happened once, it might happen again.

But if it did, that one two-legs would come save him again. The one Whiskers had dubbed Gray Muzzle.

Whiskers didn't know where Gray Muzzle had come from. Or how he'd found Whiskers. Maybe he'd been sent by Rumble Voice. Maybe he'd been sent by Bast herself.

Either way, he'd come. And he would come again.

Whiskers felt certain about that, once he thought about it. In fact, he realized he'd known it was true from the moment he'd first looked into Gray Muzzle's eyes on the Day of Weak Sunbeams.

If Whiskers needed Gray Muzzle, Gray Muzzle would come.

And knowing that, sleep came easy once again.

<<<<>>>>

SIGN UP FOR STEFON'S NEWSLETTER

Stefon loves to keep in touch with his readers, and loves to keep you reading. The best way for him to do both is for you to sign up for his newsletter.

Sign up at http://www.stefonmears.com/join

If you sign up for Stefon's newsletter, you get...

- Monthly updates about his publishing and travel schedules
- His latest news, in brief, and answers to reader questions
- A free short story for signing up
- List-only offers and occasional specials
- Plus a free short story every month!

ABOUT THE AUTHOR

Stefon Mears would go to great lengths to save a cat. Stefon has more than thirty novels to his credit, and he never stops writing. He earned his M.F.A. in Creative Writing from N.I.L.A., and his B.A. in Religious Studies (double emphasis in Ritual and Mythology) from U.C. Berkeley. He's a lifelong gamer and fantasy fan. Stefon lives in Portland, Oregon, with his wife and three cats.

Look for Stefon online:
www.stefonmears.com
himself@stefonmears.com